Revenge In Tascosa

By

Paul L. Thompson

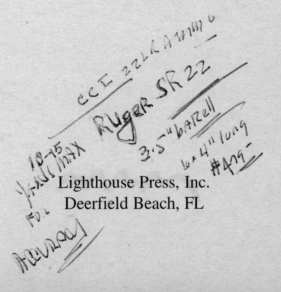

Lighthouse Press, Inc.
Deerfield Beach, FL

Lighthouse Press, Inc.
P.O. Box 910
Deerfield Beach, FL 33443
www.LighthouseEditions.com

Revenge In Tascosa

ISBN: 0-9676354-9-7

Cover Art: Mythic Studio, St. Johnsbury, VT
          www.MythicStudio.com

Harmon

Paul L. Thompson

FORWARD

U.S. Marshal M D (Shorty) Thompson's, oversized ranch partner, Buffalo, talked Shorty into letting him come along on this assignment in west Texas. James (Buffalo) Blackburn could be as stubborn as a sick mule about most everything. President Hayes, sent Shorty a wire, that had to be delivered by the Butterfield Stage Lines, telling him to head for Tascosa, and round up some rustlers and land grabbers. A nagging feeling hit Buffalo to go along, not knowing this could lead them to the killers of his wife. Law or no law, nothing will stop Buffalo from ripping them apart, limbs from body. He had waited too long to get his hands on these two low life murdering polecats.

The local Ranchers around Tascosa had waited long enough for the Texas Rangers to show up, and Washington didn't seem to give a damn. Now they would take the matter into their own hands. Too much blood had been spilled in and around Tascosa, and all of it was theirs. Friends and fellow ranchers were being shot down every day, and their cattle and property taken over by the King. Using their guns, and every farmer and rancher in the panhandle, things were about to change. King or no damn King, a lot of men were about to die!

After being kidnapped and held for five months, Sherilea Bessmer escapes from the gang of outlaws. The only thing that kept her alive was her thoughts of revenge. She had a long time to think, and her choice of weapons will be, one sharp kitchen knife, and one wooden clothespin.

CHAPTER ONE

By the time Jack Johnson and eleven of his men rode into Tascosa, with rifles in their hands, Jack's jaw was tired from being clamped tight. They had just found a neighboring rancher's body. The house and barn was burning, when one of Johnson's ranch hands saw the smoke. By the time help arrived, Ole Hanson was dead. He had been shot ten times, right in the chest. The only thing left for Johnson and his men to do, was bury Ole. Ole's wife and children were nowhere about. They were gone, as were the cattle and horses.

Johnson must now find Mrs. Hanson, and the children, before the King sends them packing with nothing but the clothes on their backs. Ole Hanson, like all the other ranchers in the area, was always a good neighbor, and didn't deserve being shot down like a dog.

Pulling to a halt in front of Doctor Gordon's house, Jack turned to his men. "Y'all keep both eyes open. If you see any of that dumb Chinaman's men, gun 'em down like the pole-cats they are. Don't wait to call me or anybody else, just gun them where you see 'em. This stealing and killing is going to stop if I have to hire a hundred men to blow those bastards to hell and back!"

Dismounting, Jack walked up the short walkway, then knocked on the front door. Doctor Gordon had a dishtowel over his left shoulder as he answered the door. "Evening, Jack. What brings you so far from home, this late in the day?"

Jack removed his hat as he stepped through the door. "Don't mean to bother you and the misses, but we just found Ole Hanson's body, down by his burned out barn. His wife and kids was gone, so I thought I'd better come on into town and make sure they made it to Carters, all right. Doc, that makes five of my neighbors that have been killed, their stock run off and their places burned. I've had about damn nigh enough, and am going to send to Dodge City for hired guns. If I can get as many as fifty, or so, I think we can take our country back. Any comment?"

Doc Gordon finished drying the last few dishes, before putting away the towel. Turning to Johnson, he had a worried look on his face. "Jack, you know by doing that, more local men are going to die. If I was you, I'd head on over to Hays City, or even Saint Joseph, and send a wire to Washington D.C. The Government of this country has got to know what's going on. We can not have rustlers and murderers running around killing and putting fear into the citizenry of west Texas."

"Doc, you know it didn't do no damned good when I sent my man all the way to Austin. The answer we got back was to tell us they didn't have enough Rangers to send all the way to the panhandle. I think we're all alone on this whole kit and caboodle. Texas, nor the US Government gives a damn!"

"All I'm saying is, who's going to stop the hired guns from taking over where the King's men leave off? Jack, please, at least try Washington first. Surely someone there will listen."

Jack let out a great sigh, and sat down at the table. "All right Doc. You draft the letter, and I'll personally take it to Saint Joseph. Dodge City would be a lot closer, and save me a weeks riding. If I only knew for sure that the telegraph operator wadn't a King's man, I could send it from there. Hell I just might put a bullet in his head to be safe, and send it anyway. But I guess I'll try Hays City first. And while we're waiting for an answer, we'll see how many more are dead around here. You know how damned slow the government is. Just to get an answer from them Washington idiots could take months. I don't believe they know we're even here, and couldn't care less."

Doc Gordon poured them coffee, before getting paper and pen. "Jack, why don't you send a couple of your men to the Carter's and check if Mrs. Hanson and the kids are there? Oh, and you may's well tell your men to go on and eat. We'll be awhile writing this letter. I'll fix you a bite here. My wife isn't back from her evening ride, so we won't be disturbed."

"Yeah, I was wondering why you was doing dishes. You do suppose she's all right, don't you? It's nigh on to sundown."

"Yes, yes, she's fine. Now and again, she just likes riding late. It's much cooler, this time of day."

"I'll send all of my men, and have them get us rooms at the hotel. We'll stay the night." Johnson was dead tired.

After much heavy thought, this letter was drafted.

'To the President of the United States, and maybe even the War Department. We, the citizens, ranchers and farmers of west Texas Panhandle, particularly in the Tascosa area, need the help of the law. Our people are being killed, and our cattle stolen. We have already and repeatedly, asked the Texas Rangers for help, but to no avail. As you know, Texas is a very large state, and the Rangers are so few. Perhaps you have a U.S. Marshal that could lend us a hand? Or, we would gladly accept the help of your Cavalry, as there are several Army Forts in the New Mexico Territory, which are within a few days ride of here.

Your immediate attention to this matter would be greatly appreciated. Please answer with a message of help, or with your decline to this situation.

Sincerely, a community in need;
Wilford T. Gordon, Doctor of medicine
Tascosa, Texas
Jack Johnson, Rancher
Tascosa, Texas

"Doc, do you think there is any chance we'll get help?"

"Get help with what, Mr. Johnson?" Rebecca had walked in and was listening to the letter, as her husband was reading it again, slowly. "Surely, neither of you think the President gives a darn or a sick owl hoot about this wide open country? There is nothing out here, except, cattle, horses, snakes, wolves, and oh, yes, wind, and more wind. Goodness gracious, there is nothing here for the government to be interested in. Not the people or this town. We do not have enough votes at election time."

Doctor Gordon looked over the top of his glasses, saying, "now, now dear. We don't know why the rangers couldn't help us. We must try the U.S. Government. That is our only hope of saving this country from those cut-throat, murdering savages."

Rebecca smiled. "All I'm saying, darling, is I wouldn't count on help of any kind. Only big money would get their attention."

Jack stood, with his hat in his hand. "Doc, give me the letter. I'll see it off to Washington, myself. And Rebecca, if the Government won't help, I swear, I'll hire every man from here to Dodge City, and plumb to the Rio Grande, that will fight. I am not going to stand by and see everything we've worked for, destroyed, and, or stolen. Enough is enough and too much.

"Well, goodnight to the both of you. I'll be well on the road, come morning. And Doc, if for some reason I don't make it back, don't you give up. You use my money, cattle and land to fight with. Just see that Maxcine is taken care of."

Maxcine

Before Doc Gordon could say a word, Rebecca shot back. "Well that is certainly what you are going to do, get your fool self killed! Why don't you just forget Washington, go on home and defend your own ranch, let this mess blow on over. I'm sure when those terrible men get what they want, they will just leave. My goodness, what else could they want?"

"Ma'am, I can't quit. The rustlers won't 'til they got it all. When they went and killed my first neighbor, they'd already gone too far. Now they have killed five. Stealing cattle is a hanging offence, killing my neighbors is asking for a bullet!"

Rebecca changed her attitude, and smiled. "But Mr. Johnson, isn't it true that they have left you and your ranch pretty much alone? Except for a few head of cattle stolen now and then, that is. I mean, goodness gracious, you're alive! Please stay that way, for Maxcine's sake!"

"Mrs. Gordon, Maxcine does matter, but my neighbors do too! Goodnight, Ma'am, Doc. I'll be heading for Hays City."

Doctor Gordon watched Rebecca, as she looked after Johnson. Her eyes were flashing mad, and her jaws were set tight, while her hands were on her hips.

"Dear, why has all this gotten you so upset?"

Rebecca was so mad, she was almost screaming. "Why? Why? Because all men are stupid, and can't leave well enough alone, that's why! They can't see past their stupid noses and want to take the law into their own hands! Every lasting one of them will wind up dead!"

"Come Dear, I have your supper in the warmer. After you eat, maybe you'll feel better."

"I don't want to feel better! Let's pick up and leave this God forsaken country. There's nothing holding us here. When the cattle stealing, land grabbing crooks are gone, we'll come back and start over. We can buy, or take over any abandoned ranch."

"But dear, these are my friends. What would they do without a doctor? My family was among the first to arrive in this small town. In fact, by me coming here as a Doctor, we helped make Tascosa. No, dear, I must stay for as long as I'm needed."

"Well you just do that! Maybe I'll stay, and maybe I won't! You seem to think more of this town and it's people, than you do me! Or maybe it's that daughter of yours that doesn't want to leave. Is that it?"

"Now dear, you're just upset."

"Yes, hell yes I'm upset!"

CHAPTER TWO

Shorty, while talking over the back his big dun, threw his saddle on the horse. "Damnit, Buffalo, I don't know when I'll be back. This dispatch from President Hayes, says I gotta go over in the Texas panhandle and talk to some big rancher, and even a Doctor. Says here it's about some cow thieves that's cutting the herds, and running the cattle over into Dodge City, Kansas.

From there they're shipping the cattle by train to Chicago. Ever where in the hell that is. I've been told it's in a state up in the northwest. Illinois, I believe I was told at one time. Yeah, Chicago is in Illinois. Looks like their also killing a lot of folks and maybe stealing the land. Now being as I'm the only U.S. Marshal this side of hell, I gotta go, no matter where."

Buffalo looked like a whipped pup. "Darn it all to heck, Shorty. You told me that we was going back up to Wyoming and get some more of my gold. Now by golly you've been telling me that for nigh on to two years. I'll be a sorry whipped mule if I ain't been working my rump off around here so we could go. Think maybe we ought'a get it done fore winter sets in?"

"Yeah Buffalo, I think we ought'a go before winter, but I took an oath, and I'm gonna stick to it until I quit, or I get my ass fired for not doing my job. 'Sides that, we ain't broke. Hell, I know we still got over four million dollars in that Denver bank. No more than we spend, that ought'a at least last a few life times. The only money of any size we've spent is for fencing this ranch, and stocking it up with horses and cattle. I've got to go, but as soon as I get back, we'll hook 'em for Wyoming. Is that all right with you? I mean, I'm sure we'll still have plenty of time."

"Dad-gum-it Shorty, I know we ain't broke! I just wanted to get away from here for awhile, to make sure there are other people alive in the world 'cept us and the hired hands. And too, I'd like to see if my gold is still there. Somebody might'a found, or stumbled on to it, you know."

Buffalo's eyes brightened, as he got a big smile on his face. "Hey, I've got one hell of an idea! Why don't I just go with you now? And when you're done with that rancher, and all that rustling, we can head on from there. The west Texas panhandle is one hell of a lot closer to Wyoming than southwestern New Mexico Territory. Who knows, you might even need some help on this one. You know, like a deputy. You've used me before, and I feel as if I need to go on this one. You know, just a terrible naggin' feeling."

"Yeah, you are one hell of a nag, but maybe that wouldn't be such a bad idea. But, do you think it wise for both of us to be gone from the ranch that long? Could be months you know. You know how these jobs are, and on top of that, what if we both get killed? Wouldn't nobody around here know it for years."

"That's it! I knew it! You just don't want me to go with you, by darn! What difference would a few weeks one-way or the other make? And if Jim can't run this place while we're gone, I'll sure as hell fire him when we get back! If we both get killed, it won't matter one damn bit what happens to this ranch!"

"All right, Buffalo, damnit! All right! I'll be damned if you ain't worse than some mangy old woman! Bitch, bitch, gripe, gripe, nag, nag! Get your gear, and your horse, unless you're going to walk! I'm already a month late, according to this dispatch. We've gotta move, now!"

An hour later, the apprehensive Shorty, and his happy partner left their Fort Tularosa ranch. Heading east, it would take them just short of two days of easy riding to reach the new silver mining boomtown of Kelly. Then it would take at least four or five more to Tascosa. The

13

mountains around the ranch were about seventy five hundred feet elevation and the St. Augustine Plains they must cross before reaching Kelly, were about fifty five hundred feet. Years ago buffalo herds kept this tall grass nibbled to within a few inches of the ground. But with the buffalo gone, the grass is belly high on a tall horse, and hides rocks and boulders that could cripple any fast moving animal.

In Shorty's mind, he knew this was a hell of a time of year to be horseback, this far from cover. Summer thunder storms with hailstones the size of horse turds, were just about an every day occurrence. He wished he'd brought his heavy elk hide robe.

Behind them, and to the southwest, Shorty saw huge thunderheads building black and strong. "Buffalo, I don't see your rain slicker. You got it, don't you? I mean, look to the southwest. Boy, them clouds are churning, we could be in for it."

"Yeah, I've got it right… well I'll be damned! I must have left it hanging on the stall in the barn. Think we can find some sort of cover in them low hills over there to the southeast?"

"Yeah, there's a pretty good sized mine tunnel just under that bluff you can see from here. We'd better kick these horses out a bit. We're about to get our asses wet. I'm sure glad we stuck to the stage road, instead of cutting across country. At least we haven't injured a horse."

They rode the horses under a large over-hang at the base of the bluff, just as huge rain-drops begin slowly falling. As each drop hit the ground, a small puff of dust scattered out-ward. An hour from now the dust would be a muddy mess.

Shorty's dun, gave a quick short, nicker. Shorty quickly stepped from the saddle. "Pssst, Buffalo, look at these tracks. Looks as if somebody has already beat us here. Look, over there, under that next over-hang, looks like a pole corral with three unsaddled horses. Get down and keep an open eye. I'm gonna see who we'll be imposing upon. I don't think they've heard us yet. Just you be ready for anything."

Buffalo dismounted and held both sets of reins. From the corner of his eye, he spotted movement, and heard a noise in the brush to his left, about two hundred feet away. "Pssst, Shorty! Hey, Shorty!"

Shorty was around the short bend, peek-ing into the mine tunnel and didn't hear Buf-falo. He had already pulled his .45, as he stepped into the darkened mine. Fifteen or twenty feet ahead, he saw light, and moved toward it, slowly.

Meantime, Buffalo had dropped the bridle reins, and pulled his .44 from the holster. Raindrops were now falling harder and harder. Holding his gun level, he headed for the noise. Yard after yard he strained his eyes, seeing slight movement from time to time, he moved ever closer. There, that same noise again. Was it a bear snorting and grunting? Slowly rounding the bush, his eyes met another set of eyes that were about waist high. Both Buffalo and the man taking a dump, shouted at the same time. "Aaaah shit!"

"What tha hell?" The man fell backward into his on pile. With his mouth open, Buffalo stepped back, as the man started cussing about falling into his own mess.

"You dirty son of a bitch! What do you mean, slipping upon a feller what's taking a crap? No privacy anymore a'tall! Now get, damnit, 'till I clean myself up! What the hell you doing with your gun out? Gonna shoot a man whats taking a dump? As a matter of fact, what in the hell are you doing here, anyway? Scaring the living hell out of a man is what you're doing! Be damned if this don't beat all! Gettin' suh damn crowded a man can't shit out in open country!!"

Buffalo stammered and hum-hawed around, then put away his gun. "Well, me and my partner saw this mine, and was about to get out of the rain. Then I heard you fart, not knowing it was a fart at the time, and came looking. And... you did fart like a sick mule you know. I'll head back over to the horses, and wait. Shorty's over the other way, towards the mine somewheres."

"No need waiting by your horses in the damn rain. There's coffee on the fire inside, but you'd better holler that your coming in, or you're labile to get your ass shot off. I'll be in, in a minute. Tell the boys I sent you. By the way, I'm sheriff Enoch, from Kelley. Who might you be?"

"Buffalo Blackburn. I'm the Deputy to U.S. Marshal Shorty Thompson. We're from the old Fort Tularosa Ranch."

"The hell you say! I didn't know Shorty had hisself a big assed nosy deputy." Enoch was still cleaning himself.

"Well, he's got one now, and I ain't nosy! Just cautious, is what I am! I'm gone, see you in the mine." Buffalo was more than a little bit riled at being called nosy.

Shorty was just coming out of the mine to help Buffalo with the horses. "Not talking to yourself, are you Buffalo?"

"No! I'm not talking to myself! I was talking to sheriff Enoch. Hell, I'm not like you, always talking to yourself!"

"Where's he at? I don't see nobody but you?"

"In the bushes, Shorty! He's taking a dump!"

"All right, then lets you and me put these

horses with theirs, over in that pole corral. We'll probably have to stay the night here. It looks as if this rain will keep up for a spell. Let's go ahead and take all our gear in. Enoch's two deputies are in there fixing something to eat. Said they'd make enough for us. I told them as much as you eat, they'd most likely have to kill one of their horses. Maybe even two."

"Thanks a hell of a lot, Shorty!"

"What in the hell are you two arguing about? Half the damn county can hear you." Jobe Enoch had walked up, pulling his rain slicker tighter around his shoulders.

Shorty smiled, saying, "howdy, Jobe. If Buffalo gives me any more lip, I may have to drown him."

Buffalo stammered and tried to have a running fit. "Me give you lip! If you wadn't my partner, I'd, I'd, well, hell forget it. Let's get in there and eat. I'm half starved. I ain't eat nothing but a few strips of jerky since breakfast."

After the meal was over, the fire was built up a bit, and the men sat around, talking. Jobe said he and his men were looking for claim jumpers, and saw the storm coming. Knowing about the abandon mine, they moved in for the night.

"Boy, Shorty, when you got rid of that damn Dunhill and his crooked assed bunch, I thought all of this crap would stop. It seems when you catch one asshole, there's two more to take his place. Where abouts are you and Buffalo off to?"

"We're headed over to Tascosa. Rustlers are hitting that ranch of old Jack Johnson's pretty hard, and he ain't been able to stop 'em. He must have mucho pull with some big shot politician, 'bout like a Senator, to get President Hayes to send a U.S Marshal to help him out. But again, they might not have local law in them parts. They figger this outlaw bunch might be headquartered all the way over in Kansas, or even Illinois. Damn, but I'd hate to go that far to catch some cow thief.

Jobe poured himself another cup of coffee before saying, "you know Shorty, I heard the number one and two outlaws in them parts was a couple of bad hombres what was running with Dunhill, when you busted up that silver scam."

Buffalo cut right into the conversation. "You wouldn't happen to have heard their names, would you?"

"Yeah, Gator Jones and Booger Boggs. I don't remember either of them, but maybe y'all do."

Shorty looked over at Buffalo. "Yeah, we know who the hell they are. They both jumped on a boat for China when we caught Dunhill's partner in San Francisco. Gator and his bunch killed Buffalo's wife, and tried to burn down our ranch. Beings as you think they might be tied up in this rustling, we'll push on pretty hard for Tascosa, come morning."

Buffalo's eyes were misty, as he told Shorty, "I knowed there was a reason I needed to come along on this job with you. Shorty, if God allows, I'm killing both of them. But, they will suffer first. This I've sworn to Kathline, and I'll keep that promise."

Shorty didn't reply to that, he only stated, "it's right close to four days ride from here, maybe even five, not killing our horses. We'll make it, and by damned, those two will not jump on a boat, this time. We'll get 'em. Ease your mind, we'll get 'em."

Shorty sure did feel sorry for Buffalo. He loved his wife more than life, and then a bunch of low life skunks killed her. It would take years for him to get over it, if ever.

They both had a restless night, thinking of how close they were to the murdering bastards that had killed Buffalo's wife.

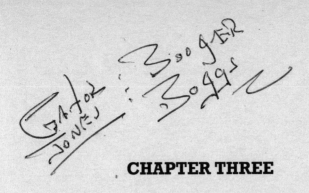

CHAPTER THREE

Continuing with two more long days of hard riding, Shorty and Buffalo made it to Fort Sumner, still in the New Mexico territory. After leaving their horses in the livery, where they would be watered and fed, Buffalo said, "I'm headed for the saloon. Sure hope you're ready for a few beers."

"Buffalo, I ain't staying in here very long. Maybe two beers, then I'm eating supper and hitting the hay pretty damn quick. And I figger..." Before Shorty could finish what he was about to say, he drew his .45 one split second after a bullet zipped past an ear. Pulling the trigger at lightening speed, both bullets found their mark. Quick Martinez was slammed back and under a table.

Walking over to the body, Shorty kicked him in the ribs, just to make sure he was dead. "Boy howdy, that little shit like to have got me that time. He must have thought I was still after him for killing his father-in-law. Hell, that's been so long ago, I most forgot. I'd say nigh on to four years have passed."

Buffalo still had his hand on his gun butt. "Damn, Shorty, next time, warn me a dab ahead of time. I damn near crapped my britches. Now, lets get a beer and supper."

The beer was luke warm, and tasted as if it the glasses hadn't been washed for about a year. Buffalo downed his in two gulps, hollering for another. Shorty had only taken a sip of his, when through the door came a rather large man with a badge pinned to his sloppy shirt front. Glancing all around the bar for a moment, he shouted, "All right, who murdered this man? Speak up now! Don't make me hunt you out!"

Shorty couldn't believe his ears, but stood and said, "by damned I killed him! And it sure's hell wasn't murder!"

"Now son, we'll let a jury decide that. Turn over your gun, and I won't have to kill you here and now." The town marshal had his hand on his gun butt, as if he wanted Shorty to draw against him. "Come on, come on, boy! I don't have all day! I've got to get you to jail, then head home for supper."

Shorty was getting ticked off pretty damn quick. "Look, Marshal, I'm a..." Before he could finish his sentence, the marshal put himself into a drawing stance.

"Boy, if I have to gun you down, I will!"

"Mister, if that gun of yours moves one quarter inch in your holster, you'll eat so much lead, your head will fall through your asshole! I am a United States Marshal, and that little dead shit on the floor over there, took a shot at me as soon as I walked through the door! Now get your hand away from that gun butt where we can talk, or be stupid, and go for it all the way!"

The town marshal had bluffed about as far as he could, and knew it. Sweat popped up under his eyes, and he swallowed hard. "Just how, now how, I mean, how am I suppose to know you're a U.S. Marshal? You look mighty young to me."

"If you ain't blind, and can see this far, there is a star on my chest. That would be a good place to start." Shorty frowned.

"Well yes, I can see that far, but what if it ain't yours?"

"Then that means I killed somebody a hell of a lot faster with a gun than you'll ever be to get it! Now move your damn hand away from your gun...now!" Shorty was through talking.

"Uh, uh, me being the law, and all, I don't think I should do that. People of the town might think me a coward."

Shorty drew his gun so fast the marshal didn't see it until it was cocked and pointing dead center of his face. "Now, unbuckle your gun belt and let it drop! Now, you dumb shit! Now, do it now!" Shorty was so mad, he wanted to walk over and pistol-whip the idiot in the head. Maybe, just maybe it would knock some sense into him. "How could anyone so stupid be wearing a badge? Why would anyone so stupid, wear a badge?"

Shorty was so mad he was about to start stuttering.

The gun and belt dropped to the floor with a loud clunk "Now back off!" Shorty picked up the marshal's gun and belt, handing it to the barkeeper. "Barkeep, if you give him back this gun before I leave town, after I kill him, I'll come after you! You got that? That son-of-a-bitch is stupidly dangerous."

The bartender swallowed hard and said, "yes Sir, Marshal Shorty. I hear you loud and clear. No gun for him until you leave town, or you're killing us both. Uh huh, yeah, I got that, killing us both is what you said."

Shorty looked back at the bartender in a hurry. "You know me? From where?'

"You and Sheriff Pat Garret came in here a few months ago. Remember? You was talking to a couple of cowboys, Bob and Elmore, then they left and Sheriff Garret came in. Y'all sat right over there at that table and had a couple of beers. I brung your beer myself, remember? Oh, and later I heard Elmore was killed up north. Yeah, some little kid went and dusted him. Said it was the littlest gun anybody had ever saw. Uh huh, fast!"

"Yes, I remember, but why didn't you speak up when this dumb ass like to have gotten himself filled full of holes?''

"Figgered it to be no affair of mine, if he wanted to go and get his self killed. He's from back east and really dumb about us folks out here in the west. Tries to talk everybody to death.''

Shorty looked at the overly large town marshal and asked, "didn't you tell me that you are the town marshal?''

"Yes, that is right, and I most certainly am!''

"How in the hell did you become marshal, and when?''

"I arrived in town nine days ago, just as they were putting the former marshal to rest in his grave. Oh, he was killed. His horse kicked him in the head when he bent down to remove a stone from one of his back hoofs. After the funeral, someone asked, "Who in the world will be marshal now?" Being as I was a peace officer before leaving New Jersey, I felt it my duty to serve the people of this town.''

"Mister, you'd better feel it your duty to un-serve them and turn in that badge. You'll last about as long as a good fart in a windstorm. This is out west in the territories, and is not a state. Hell, it's nowhere near New Jersey. There are some fellows in these parts that will blow you away, and piss on your body before it gets cold. Five minutes ago, I damn near done it myself, and I am a U.S. Marshal. There's just something about you that pisses everybody off. And number one, you don't listen worth a damn. And number two you still don't listen worth a damn. And number three you talk to damn much. Your mouth is going full time, and you can't hear with your mouth open."

"I see your point, Marshal. I have made several grave mistakes today. I'll be leaving now, thankful that I'm still alive." He reached and removed his badge, placing it on the bar beside his gun. "Good-day, gentlemen." He turned and walked through the bat-winged doors.

Shorty sat down for a moment, then put his hands on his knees and stood up. "Buffalo, let's eat and get to bed."

Buffalo headed for the door, stopping just short of going outside. "After you, Mister U.S. Marshal. If some other asshole takes a shot at you, I don't want to be in the way."

"Shorty laughed, "Thanks, pard', thanks a hell of a lot. But if they miss little old me, my bet is they'll get you."

They walked out into the street just as the moon slipped behind a cloud. The lights on the hotel porch seemed to brighten in the darkness. Several men were walking toward the hotel entrance as Shorty and Buffalo went inside.

"One room, two beds." Shorty laid two dollars down. "We'll be in the café for a bit, then I want a tub of hot water. I'm gonna take a bath where I can rest good tonight."

Leaving Fort Sumner, Shorty and Buffalo

rode east by northeast at a steady gallop. They could push the horses pretty hard for a few hours, but after the sun started beating down, they would slow to a walk. After riding from the Pecos River Valley, except for a few low hills now and again, they were on broad plains that seemed to stretch forever.

After a couple of hours, Shorty half stood in his stirrups, looking all around. "Boy howdy, Buffalo, anybody can sure tell why these are called the staked plains. If a feller didn't know where he was going, he'd damn sure get lost in nothing flat. Everything out here looks the same, sand, bear-grass, (yucca) and mesquite. Then a small rise can be traversed that looks the same on both sides. Then there is these same damn dry wash arroyos with the straight up sides and about ten or twelve feet deep. Fall in one of them, you've got a dead horse, and probably be killed yourself. If not that, then there you are, lost. Think you'd ever get lost, Buffalo? Really lost at all? I mean any-where, lost."

"Now Shorty, that's a damn dumb thing to ask a mountain man! I've tromped over this whole west, from Montana, clear down to Mexico. There ain't many places in the Rocky Mountain country that I ain't been. How do you think I found all of that gold up there in Wyoming? It sure as hell wasn't pointed out to me. I found it. And... found my way out and back a few times."

Shorty removed his hat to wipe the sweat from his forehead. "All right, Buffalo, I believe you. But close your eyes for a few minutes and turn around more than once, damn a feller could be lost. Anyhow, bout how long would you say we've been on the trail this morning?"

"Shorty, you've got the only watch! Look at it and see!"

"Without looking at my watch, I'd say about six hours. That would put it right at twelve o'clock. Wanna bet as to who can get the closest? Shorty smiled, trying to get a rise out of Buffalo."

"No I don't! What the hell difference does it make nohow? We still gotta ride 'til dark, then set up camp, fix supper, then lay down and go to sleep. So what the hell difference does it make what time it is? I'm asking you that! So tell me huh?"

"None, none atall. Just talking, and wanted to know how long it'd take you to get pissed off, that's all. Pretty quick, huh? Let's kick 'em out for a while. They seem rested enough."

Hours later they were riding along the top of a cap-rock, where the plains dropped off several hundred feet to rolling sand hills, grass, mesquite bushes, and one hell of a lot of cactus. "Buffalo, bet we can see fifty or sixty miles from up here. Think so? Just look across that land. Man that is a lot of nothing."

"Yeah, at least fifty miles. From here, by staying on the cap-rock, we'll make Tascosa before sundown tomorrow?"

"Yeah, that's about what I figgered, maybe even noon."

"I figger we ought'a be getting close to the Texas Panhandle within the next few hours. Instead of that, maybe we better drop off the cap-rock along here somewhere and hit that little San Jon creek. We can water the horses and maybe stay the night at the N D Ranch. From there we just follow the creek to the Canadian River, then head on east from there."

Buffalo glanced at Shorty, when he said no more. "Ever which way is the fastest to Tascosa. I've looked for this for over two years. I'm gonna let them two know it's me that's killing 'em, and why. Shorty, I know the law can frown on a man taking the law into his own hands, but these two got it coming. After I'm done with 'em, you can lock me up, hang me, or whatever you have to. It won't matter what happens to me after I get 'em."

Shorty watched Buffalo's face. "Naw, law or no law, I'm helping you get these two, Buffalo. They both need killing, real bad. The only way we can't is if they give up, with no gun. You know what I mean, hands in the air."

Buffalo looked at Shorty and grinned. "I sure hope that's what they do. I want to beat them to death with my bare hands."

After staying the night at the N D Ranch, they arrived in Tascosa five hours before sundown the next afternoon. Buffalo asked Shorty, "What day of the week and month is this? Boy there sure is a lot of saddle horses at the hitch rails. No bigger than this place is, I'd say everybody rode two or three horses."

Shorty leaned forward in his saddle to rest his bottom. "Today is Friday the third of June. What makes this little place so busy is it's one of the few places to get a drink in the west Texas Panhandle. Closest other town is north of here over in Kansas. Although in Oklahoma Indian Strip, there is a couple of trading post. Beaver is one of them and then..." Buffalo cut in.

"Damn, Shorty, I was just wondering why this place was so busy. I don't need to know every watering hole this side of the big river. But beings as you're talking, where do we find that rancher, Johnson? I'd like to find Gator and his partner, now."

"Let's get a room and bath, then head over to the saloon. Maybe Johnson or some of his hands will be in town for the dance. If not, somebody will know the way to his ranch."

The fellow behind the desk at the hotel was so skinny he could have hid behind a fence post. "Y'all fellers jest got here in tha nick ah time. Two or so more hours and you'd been out of luck on gettin' a room. As it is, I only got one left, and it's jest got one bed. Hope y'all don't mind sleepin' together, cause tonight, you are."

"Naw, we ain't!" Shorty turned to Buffalo. "You can have the room. I'll go to the barbershop and get a bath and shave. Then tonight I'll sleep in the hayloft at the livery. Go on Buffalo, you take the room. I'll see you in the saloon after my shave and bath. Just don't drink all the beer, I'll be needing a couple."

An hour later Shorty walked through the swinging batwing doors at the Badlands Saloon. Spotting Buffalo at a poker table, he picked himself up a beer at the bar and headed that way.

"Marshal, over here!"

A small rancher looking fellow had called out to Shorty. Turning to see who had shouted, Shorty bumped into a table and spilled several drinks. Mad cowboys were jumping to their feet, cussing and wanting to whip somebody's ass.

As Shorty apologized, one cowboy let his fist fly toward the side of Shorty's head. The blow never connected. Another one of the men brought a cane down hard across the flying forearm before it got to Shorty.

With a squall of pain and surprise, the cowboy grabbed his arm. "What in the hell did you do that for, Buckner? I'd have assholed this little bastard for spilling our drinks."

"Yeah, and more than likely got yourself

shot, and if not killed, at least fired. Yeah, I'd have fired you. Now sit your ass down and be still, the man didn't do it mean like."

Shorty saw, and heard all of this take place, but didn't let it bother him, and walked on over to the table of the man that had hollered out. "Howdy, I'm Shorty Thompson. Do I know you?"

"Sit down, Marshal. I'll have us another drink brought over. Naw, you don't know me, but I know you. Well, at least I know your brother, Ben. And y'all do look one hell of a lot alike. Ben might out weigh you thirty or so pounds, but you're still a Thompson. I'm Dean Bessmer. I've got me a little two-cow outfit up north towards the Oklahoma strip. Well I did have a few cows until them damn rustlers wiped me plumb out. They got damned near every head of cattle I've got. Got my ass, had! Bet they didn't leave me fifty head. I'm down here at Tascosa to team up with the other local ranchers to form us a lynching posse. We'll have nigh on to a hundred men ready to ride in just a matter of a few days. Johnson said he'd sent all the way to Washington for help, but had about give up on getting it. Been nigh on to two months ago. Are you it, or just passing through?"

"Well, I reckon I'm it, if y'all are with Johnson. My dispatch said I needed to get in touch with him, and a Doctor Gordon. Does anyone have any idea who, and how many are

32

involved in the rustlings?"

"Yeah, we sure's hell do! But I'd better keep my trap shut 'till Jack gets here. You see, I'm still a little pissed off about loosing everything I had. Jack doesn't want me going off half-cocked and getting myself and crew killed. We'll wait. Jack says if I do, maybe we can get some of my stock back. He's already sent... Well shit fire, I just can't keep my mouth shut!"

Shorty was now sitting at Dean's table, sipping his beer. "Do you know when Johnson is showing up here, or is he? And... who did he send where? And will it get 'em killed? I'd like to see him before you fellows go out and maybe hang the wrong men. Not saying you would, just that you could."

"Yeah, Jack won't be in until tomorrow late. He's sitting up a trap that should work. If not, we'll still get to kill us a bunch of them rustling bastards, and maybe put a stop to the whole damn gang. And believe me, it ain't the wrong men. We, we hell, ever'body knows who's behind this end of the rustling. Thieving bastards. It's gonna be tough, but if done right, it'll work. Our main problem is crooked law. It has gone... There I go again, talking my fool head off. I'll just stay shut 'till Jack gets here."

Shorty took a long drink from his mug of beer, and looked back at Buffalo. Facing Dean once more, he asked, "if all along y'all have knowed who in the hell was stealing your beef, just why in the hell did you have to have a U.S. Marshal?" Seems to me if my memory serves me right, cowmen still know how to use a rope on something besides a steer."

"Yeah, we sure's hell do, but... Damnit, you'll just have to wait for Jack. He'll clue you in on everything. He's running it."

Shorty started to say something more, but Buffalo bumped him on the left arm. "Hey Shorty, we gotta talk somewhat on all this." When Shorty just sat there, Buffalo loudly said, "Well!"

Shorty half turned and looked up. "Well, what?"

"Damnit Shorty, I said, we need to talk, now! And not here! Let's go outside where we won't be overheard. Can you hurry?"

"Yeah, yeah, I can hurry, but I don't see the damn rush. Jack Johnson ain't gonna be in town 'till nigh on to dark tomorrow."

"Shorty! Just get the hell up and come on!" Buffalo wasn't mad, just in one hell of a hurry to talk. Once outside, he couldn't hold it back. "Damnit Shorty, Johnson is what I needed to talk to you about and couldn't take the chance of anybody overhearing. You saw them fellers I was sitting and taking with? Well, anyway, they told me that Johnson was stirring up too much trouble, and the rustlers was going to hit him on his way into Tascosa tomorrow mornin'. They figger if they kill the biggest rancher in these parts the smaller ones will just drop their drawers and squat and pee. You know, no more problems, least wise that's what they hope. Them fellers didn't know where he's gonna get killed though. One of 'em overheard two fellers talking about it, saying it was gonna happen. Not by these men, but by somebody else."

Shorty looked back through the saloon window, hoping to see if the fellow's Buffalo had been sitting with, and if they had moved. They hadn't. "All right, just who in the hell are those men that they'd know so much about what's about to happen to Johnson? And why in the hell hadn't they let him know?"

"They all work for the Spider Box outfit. They're waiting for their boss to get here. Then one of them decided it was too late, and he wasn't coming. He's supposed to join up with Johnson tomorrow, at his place. From what they said, the Spider Box is between here and Johnson's ranch. Johnson's headquarters is east of here along the Canadian, but wraps all the way south and west to the New Mexico Territory line. It borders the N D Ranch on the east and north. One hell of a big spread."

Shorty thought for a couple of minutes before saying, "let's go back in and talk with Dean Bessmer. He might know the owner of the Spider Box bunch. Yeah, uh huh, shor' is funny that these fellers are sitting here on their rumps when a friend, and rancher neighbor is about to go and get hisself killed. And ta'boot, their boss is riding down the same trail at about the same time. And coming to the same meeting… I'd say something else besides rotten butter-milk stinks around here. Yeah, better talk to Dean real fast like. I think time's short for saving both of those men."

Buffalo reached for, and took Shorty's beer mug. "I'll refill this and get me another. Meet you at Dean's table." Buffalo headed for the bar, while Shorty worked his way through men and between tables.

Upon reaching Dean's table, Shorty saw several men he hadn't seen before, sitting and playing cards. Dean wasn't around. Looking at other tables, he knew this was where Dean had been sitting just moments before.

"Excuse me, fellers, but did any of y'all see where Dean Bessmer upped and run off to. I just left here, and he had told me he would wait 'till I got back."

Of the four men at the table, only one of them raised his eyes enough to see Shorty. "Nope, don't know no Dean Bessmer. Wadn't nobody sitting here, when we moved in and sat down. Now move it, you're interfering with a poker game. Don't like my game being throwed off."

Shorty glanced to the next table and recognized the men as the ones that were there earlier. Turning to talk, he thought better and walked around to the other side, where he was facing the table where Dean had been. "Hey fellers, y'all didn't happen to see what happened to Dean, did you? Or when he'll be back?"

Two of the men dropped their eyes to their cards, pretending not to hear. Both other men looked to the next table before one of them spoke. "Naw, he didn't say nary a word. Just finished his drink and walked off towards the back door. Might'a went to the outhouse. You can sit if you like, and see if he comes back. Hadn't been gone that long." All the while he was talking, he was using his left foot to tap Morris code against the chair Shorty had his hand on. His eyes found Shorty's twice the whole time, then returned to his own cards. He never glanced at the other table, or the men sitting there.

Shorty had caught the pleading expression on the fellow's face, but didn't understand what it was about until the Morris code began to take effect on his mind. When the code tapping quit, Shorty tipped his hat. "Well thanks anyway fellers. I need to..."

Buffalo walked up, handing Shorty his beer. "Where'd Dean run off to? Wadn't he setting right there?"

Shorty took his beer saying, "yeah, but something must have come up, and he had to leave. We may's well ride on out toward his place. We might even run into him or even Jack."

Shorty and Buffalo went out the front door, and to the hitch-rail. Buffalo kept looking over his shoulder, but Shorty went on about business as though nothing was wrong, or was going to be. Taking the dun's reins, he knew Buffalo was taking too long. "Buffalo, get your horse and walk him to the water trough. I'm headed that way, but will stop beside the building and remove a rock from Dunnie's forefoot. Then I'll be at the water trough."

"Hell, Shorty, if Dunnie's got a stone, why don't you get it out here? Seems to me that's the sensible thing to do."

"Damnit Buffalo, I didn't ask you what was or was not sensible! Now get your damn horse and head for the water trough!" Shorty was already walking toward the end of the saloon walkway, where from the alley a hat brim could be seen.

As Buffalo and his paint walked past, headed for water, Shorty had the dun's right foreleg between his knees. Using his knife, Shorty was working at an unseen object, while listening to a man from the alley.

"Mister, if you are a Marshal like I heard you was, pay a lot of mind to what Dean was telling you. I know for a fact... ahh, aw naw, aahhh, unhhh!"

When Shorty heard nothing else for a moment or two, without turning around, he asked, "you know what for a fact? I didn't catch that last bit. What was that?"

Hearing nothing in return, Shorty slowly glanced toward the alley. From this angle, the only thing he could see was two legs lying on the ground. Dropping the dun's hoof, he stepped around the end of the wooden walkway, and into the alley. On the ground in front of him sat the man, against the wall with a knife buried deep in his chest. Scribbled awkwardly in the dirt by his right hand was one word, *king.*

"King, king, now who or what in the hell does that mean?"

Walking back to the dun, he hollered at Buffalo. "Hey, Buffalo, come on over here while I go in the back way of the saloon. I want to see if those fellers are still at their table. Somebody went and killed this one to keep him shut. He was trying to tell me something, maybe even a warning."

Shorty entered the saloon from the back door, but didn't even get a glance from the fifty or so men that were busy drinking, and playing cards. The back door was the way to and from the outhouse, so no one thought entering from there odd. Seeing the barkeep, he leaned across the bar and asked, "did any of those men at that table over there leave by the back door for a few minutes, and just get back?"

The bartender finished pouring the drink he had in his hand before asking, "what men, at which table?"

Shorty pointed out the table, and to each man. "Now, did either of those men leave the saloon in the past ten minutes?"

"Nope, can't say that they did. Really can't say that they didn't either. Ain't had time to stand here watching that table the whole time. Been waiting on customers. What do you care where they go, or when they go? You got business with them?"

"Well somebody just killed a feller that was sitting at that table to the left of them and..." Shorty never got to finish.

The bartender came loose. "Listen here asshole! No such thing! Ain't been no killings in here tonight! Had ah been, I'd have knowed it! Now get! Get damnit, I ain't got tim..."

Shorty had him by the shirtfront and pulled half way across the bar. "Listen turd-face! I didn't say he was killed in here! He was killed in the alley beside this damn saloon. He came out to talk to me and somebody put a knife in his chest. So when somebody is talking to you, and trying to tell you something, keep the hell shut until they are finished talking! You might learn a bit! Now, do you know anybody around here by the name of King?" Shorty was tired of snotty answers.

"King, King, yep, heard of him, that's all. But I'll find out if anybody else knows him, as soon as you let go of my shirt."

Shorty released the shirtfront. "Sorry, forgot I had you half on the bar. Before you holler out that the man is dead, let's talk to his friends over there. Think you can get one of them over here without that other table getting wise? I'd hate for the these three to get killed too, just because they talked to me."

"Just who in the hell are you that would get anybody killed just for talking with you?"

"Oh, forgot to mention, I'm U.S. Marshal M D Thompson. Everybody calls me Shorty. I'm here about the cattle rustling."

The bartender just looked at Shorty. "Well, I can sure as hell believe that!"

Shorty eye balled him good. "Believe what?"

"You being called Shorty. Now don't go getting pissed off!" The bartender had both hands in front of himself, covering up.

"I'm not the sensitive type. I've been called Shorty since age eleven. Now see if you can get one of them fellers attention. Say, what in the hell's your name?"

"Arnold. And everybody calls me Arnold!" His and Shorty's eyes met for a split second, then they both grinned.

Getting three mugs of beer, Arnold waded

through men getting to the table. He spoke in a low voice. "Frank, that little feller at the bar needs to have a talk with you. Real easy like, don't want nobody to know yer talking. Wait a few minutes, then come to the bar and holler at me or something, sound pissed off."

Arnold then raised his voice. "No such damn thing! You ain't paid me nary a dime! Now finish them drinks and hit the street! Just who in the hell do you think you are, noway?"

One of the other men, with a puzzled look asked, "what in the hell's wrong with Arnold? Ain't seen him this way before."

With his left eye, where the other table couldn't see, Frank winked at his employees. "I don't know, but the bastard must be senile, I've paid him for every drink we've had. Y'all boys just sit tight, while I go straighten this out. I'll be back shortly."

Frank bellied up to the bar about three feet from where Shorty stood. Speaking fairly loud, he asked, "what's this all about, Arnold? I always pay my way as I go. You're just pissed off at something and want to take it out on me and my hands. That about right? Here's my money, now give me a beer while we talk. If you want to that is."

Shorty had edged a little closer and said in a low tone.

"Mister, that feller that was sitting with y'all, came outside to talk with me, and is now dead.

Some bastard follered him out and put a knife in his chest. Do you know what this is all about?"

"Yeah, I know what it's all about! Too damn many nosey people coming around asking fool questions! And it's gonna get a lot more men killed besides Charlie, if you don't get the hell out of here and wait 'til Johnson gets here. He's the onlyest one to talk to. Spies are everywhere, damnit, everywhere!"

Shorty wanted to get right in Frank's face for thinking it was his fault about his friend getting killed. "Look feller, I'm just trying to find out about what cattle rustling has to do with men getting killed here in town. Say, one more thing, before your friend cashed in, in the dirt beside him he wrote, 'king'. Do you have any idea what he meant by that?"

Frank's face turned a bit pale, and he stopped his beer mug half way to his mouth. "King, hell yes I kno…!" A bullet came through the window, knocking Frank into Shorty. Shorty grabbed hold, holding him up for a moment before letting him slip slowly to the floor in a small pool of blood.

Four quick shots were heard from the street as Shorty rolled Frank on his back. Frank's eyes were closed, but he said, "I'm alright, it ain't that bad. Got a blood vessel on the back of my hand is all. Just you get somebody to haul me out'a here like I was dead. I'll talk with you at the doctor's house. Now let it be known that I'm dead. Hurry damnit, right now, or I will be."

Shorty lay the bleeding hand across Frank's chest and blood soaked on to his shirtfront. It looked as if the hand was covering a large hole. Standing, Shorty removed his hat. "Poor fellers gone, not a thing can be done. Arnold, where's the Doctor's house? I'll have him took there, or is there a undertaker here bouts?"

As Arnold was telling Shorty that the Doctor was also the undertaker, Buffalo came through the door looking for Shorty.

"Hey Shorty, you alright? Some ass hole came out of the saloon and grabbed his rifle from a saddle boot, and just aimed it towards the window and fired. Guess this feller on the floor is the unlucky one that took the lead? Blowed a lung out, huh?"

"Yeah, he's it." Shorty was glad to see Buffalo. "Here, Buffalo, give me a hand and we'll get the body over to the doctors. That's the least we can do."

"But Shorty, I think we ought'a follow them fellers. I heard one of them say they had to go tell Mister King, or Buster King, anyway, something about a king, that a U.S. Marshal was in town and asking too many questions. And that too many town folk and ranchers was ready to talk to him. A feller standing in the street got off a couple of shots at 'em as they rode off, 'fore they put a slug in him. He's deader'n hell."

Shorty looked at Buffalo, "why wadn't you shooting?"

"Hell, I was all the way to the corner, and they was too many people between me and them. Seems when gunfire happens, men that could do something about it find cover, and the ones that can't, come out of the wood work."

Shorty dropped to one knee, beside Frank, saying, "Buffalo, lets get this feller to the under-taker before he starts stinking."

"Why us? Hell anybody here could do it and we could get after them fellers." Buffalo had his hands on his hips.

Shorty's eyes narrowed as he hissed at Buffalo. "Damnit Buffalo, quit questioning every-thing I say or do, or get your ass back to the ranch, and I'll get the help I need here!"

Buffalo was taken back by Shorty's harsh words. "Damn Shorty, I didn't mean to piss you off. I was just trying to help. Thought maybe them fellers might led us to Gator and Booger. Alright, let's move this feller, he don't look that heavy."

Once in the doctor's house, Frank stood up and Buffalo damn near crapped his britches. "Shit feller, I thought you was dead! Shorty, why didn't you tell me abou..."

"Because Buffalo, for some reason, today your mouth is working overtime. It's got the scours, and you talking could have gotten us all killed. This feller here, Frank, is about to tell us something to help clear up a bunch of crap."

The doctor was cleaning Frank's slight wound. "Alright Marshal, what the hell happened to Charlie? I told him not to go out and talk with you! Told him it'd get him killed, and it did!"

"Well, I never saw who done it. We was just talking, and I had my back to the alley. He started to tell me something and stopped. I turned to see his legs on the ground, then walked over and found him with a knife buried in his chest. Now, what do you know about this feller, King? It seems every time his name is mentioned somebody gets shot at. Oh, and before I forget it, where in the hell did Dean Bessmer get off to?" Shorty had found a chair and was sitting with his back to Buffalo, and an open window. Buffalo was standing with his back resting against the doorframe, wishing Shorty would hurry.

Frank looked at the doctor, then to Shorty. "Dean really did head for the outhouse, but never came back. Ain't like him to up and run from nothing. He's a tough little shit. Now this king bit is going to..." Frank slumped dead with a bullet between the eyes, just as the rifle fire echoed through the room. It was deafening. Shorty's ears were still ringing as he stumbled past Buffalo and into the street.

With dust rising high behind their horses, two men were whipping and spurring, headed toward the Canadian River. "Buffalo, let's get our horses and catch those two bastards! I'm going to find out what the hell this feller King has to do with everything around here!"

Doctor Gordon, still wiping Frank's blood from his left cheek and neck, half shouted, "Marshal, there ain't nobody named King! It's this big stupid bastard that came to town wearing a turban, and some stupid looking half shoes. They clunk like they're made out of wood. Tells every body he's a king. He's a Chinaman foreigner fellow, talks weird as hell. Came in with a couple of hard cases by the names of Gator and Booger. They're killers, nothing but murdering no good rotten, egg suckin' theiving southern carpetbaggers.

"Came to town bragging they had just got back from over the ocean. They brought this king back here with lots of money to invest in livestock, and maybe even take over some of the open range, and set up a ranching operation. King my butt, nothing but a fat assed Chinaman is all he is. That's what I'd guess. The only thing that's happened since they got here is, cattle rustling, murder, and more murder and more rustling. If it wasn't for my daughter teaching school here, we'd already be gone back to Joplin Missouri. Texas ain't got enough rangers to come and help us out. But... if these killings keep up, there won't be any kids left to be taught, then maybe I can get my daughter out of here and back where its safe. My wife seems to like these wide-open spaces, and would like to stay. Lord, but sometimes I wish my first wife was still alive. She was the mother of my grown daughter. Rebecca and I have no children."

"Doc, getting back to what's happening around here. You mean those bastards are killing kids!" Shorty almost screamed and shuttered at the very thought.

"No, no, not kids. Killing the fathers, and burning down their places, then the family moves on. You know, they go back to wherever they came from. As a matter of fact, there are two families waiting to leave now. They're staying right here in town with the Carter's. Mister and Mrs. Carter have a large home with no kids of their own. Plenty of room, and they love to help every family in need that they possible can."

"Why are they waiting to leave, if the man is dead and buried? Are the wives or any of the kids sick, or injured?" Shorty thought he might be going mad. He had never heard of such a thing. Women and kids homeless because of some cattle rustling? Maybe there is a hell of a lot more than that going on.

The Doctor was still washing blood from the chair and floor. Buffalo had helped place Frank on a low table. "Naw, Naw, they ain't none of them sick. It's just that they have to wait until that bastard called the king, decides to pay them something for what ever is left of their place. He says he's buying it, but he's going to steal it anyhow. You know, the land and maybe a few head of livestock. Perhaps a few chickens, wagon and plow. Ever what wasn't burned up in the fire, which Gator and his men set. Pitiful little is what it'll be. Anyway, giving them a little money gets them away from here. It'd probably be pretty bad if some of them wanted to stay."

"Doc, if ever body knows about this, why in the hell are they killing these men that want to talk with me? And another thing, why ain't you afraid to talk? You could be dead next."

"They need me too bad, to patch up their worthless hides when some rancher of farmer sees them coming and gets off a lucky shot. The reason they're killing every soul that talks, is the word has gotten around that you're a U.S. Marshal. Talking witnesses could get them hung. This intimidates all the people here bouts. So, no talking, no witnesses, no hangings, at least that's the way they look at it. They won't kill you unless they have to. Other law comes looking after their own, and for some reason, this bunch sure are afraid of the law."

Shorty started to walk out the door, but stopped and turned around. "But the ranchers that are having their cattle rustled will talk, won't they? I mean the ones that ain't dead. What about the women that have had their husbands murdered? Think some of them just might talk a dab?"

"Now Marshal. You know as well as I do, you can't be seen talking with those women. Their blood would be on your hands. To beat that, I might be pushing the joker too damned far, talking to you right now. They might decide they don't need me so bad after all. If I was you, I'd head for Johnson's, and at least maybe intercept him. If he's got enough men along, maybe you can keep him alive. Words about that he won't make it to Tascosa."

Shorty was thinking as fast as he could. "All right, we'll head for Johnson's, but can you tell me where this king and his men might be holing up? If I could be around when he comes to pay off these women..."

Doctor Gordon ran his hand through a full head of gray hair before saying, "Marshal, he don't come in to town much, he just sends some gun happy coward in, who throws a few dollars on the ground in front of the woman he's running off. Then he sits there on his horse and laughs like a stupid hyena, while they get on hands and knees to pick it up. When they get done, they make them sigh a piece of paper, giving their holdings to that Chinaman. The young children think that's fun, but its all mighty embarrassing to the women. Right down humiliating, and if someone else tries to help, they get run off. A couple of men were shot for trying to interfere."

The more Shorty heard, the madder he got. "Doctor Gordon, ain't there one man left around here with a set of balls? It looks to me as if the messenger would have been blowed out of his saddle, then enough men would have gotten on horses and gone after that idiot calling his self a king! Damn I can't believe this is happening in the Texas Panhandle!

"Most places we have too many citizens taking the law into their own hands, but here, where they need to, not one son of a bitch lifts one damn finger to save themselves, much less the neighbor women and her children! If not for the women and children, I'd hit that damn saddle of mine and ride the hell out of here and never look back!

"To beat that, I saw a piss poor looking jail house as we rode in. Where in the hell is your town marshal or sheriff, when all of this takes place?"

Doc Gordon stepped back a foot or two, watching Shorty's eyes. "Now Marshal, don't get so pissed off! Our sheriff was killed several months ago, and the town council was forced to name a man to take his place. We are trying to do something, that's exactly what Johnson is trying to do! He's not worried about his place and the rustling out there. Hell he's got the money to hire as many men as it takes to cover his outfit. And... he's done just that. He could stay out of all this, and be safe.

"Now he's trying to raise enough of his fellow ranchers to come in here and get rid of the damn spies. Them spy bastards are the ones that shoot people from hiding, and keep track of this town. We've got a pretty good idea who they are, and we're going to act on it when Johnson gets here. After that, they'll go after Gator and that whole rotten bunch, including the so-called king. I just hope Johnson makes it here. He had told me he was giving up on getting any help from Washington. It's been well over two months since he went to Hays City Kansas and sent that wire. Too many men have died here, it's gonna get worse."

By this time Shorty had mounted his dun, and Doctor Gordon was on the wooden walk. Shorty leaned forward in the saddle and ask, "you know for sure it wasn't some State Senator, or local politician what sent for me?"

"Oh yes, I know that for a fact. We don't have any local politicians. I helped Johnson draft the message right here on my kitchen table. Does that mean anything to you, that might help?"

"No, no, not necessarily. But..., what did you

mean awhile ago when you said the town council was forced to name a man as sheriff? Most
crooked politicians do that. Use force, I mean.
But knowing that didn't happen, has to lead
somewhere else."

"I am sure the king told them the worthless bum to appoint. I was down sick with the
flu at the time and couldn't sit in on the meeting. They didn't talk about it, too scared I'm
sure."

"I think me and Buffalo had better get on
the trail towards Johnson's place. We might
even stop by the Spider Box and talk to the
owner. Some of his men that was over at the
saloon, sure knew a lot about what's going on."

"David Snyder is his name."

"Whose name?"

"The owner of the Spider Box."

"Oh, all right, thanks. We'll see you when
we get back."

CHAPTER FOUR

Two hours on the trail towards Johnson's ranch, Shorty slowly turned his head and glanced over his left shoulder. "Buffalo, don't turn full around, but do you see a rider across the river and back about three hundred yards?"

Buffalo looked from under his hat brim, then turned completely around. "Naw, I don't see nobody. Did you?"

"Shit Buffalo, if I hadn't seen something, I wouldn't have ask you to look!" Shorty stopped the dun, and looked where he had seen the rider.

"Well I'll be damned! I'm sure I saw a rider coming on pretty fast. Maybe he saw us and hid... No, there he is, coming out of that draw. Hell, he's waving his hat for us to wait."

As the rider crossed the river, and headed straight for them, Shorty blurted out, "well I'll be damned, that's Dean Bessmer!"

Before Dean could say a word, Shorty asked, "Where in the hell did you get off to? I thought maybe that bushwhacker had took care of you too."

Dean got off his horse and preceded to take a leak, saying, "damn, but I've needed to do that for over an hour. Naw, the bastards didn't get me, but I sure as hell got one of them. While I was waiting for you, I got up and went to the outhouse. When I got done and headed back, a couple of fellers came running out of the alley and mounted their horses. They kicked the hell out of them leaving, so I figgered they had been up to no good. I follered them plum to Mullins old ranch. Man, oh man, it had been mor'n two years since I'd been out there. That damn so called king, and his bunch have got thousands and thousands of cattle hid in that big valley, just north of the river. Looks like they might be getting ready to head to Kansas with them.

"Them two old boys I follered, spotted me taking a look and came after me. I had a running gunfight for a half hour or so before I got a lucky shot and knocked one of them out of his saddle. The other'n stopped his chase, must'a figgered it unsafe.

"Anyhow, when I got back to the saloon, Arnold told me y'all was at Doc Gordon's. I got to Doc's, and he told me Charlie and Frank was dead, and y'all was headed to Johnson's. Not knowing what else to do, I headed after you, hoping to help."

Shorty and Buffalo both got off their horses to take a leak. Shorty turned his head over his shoulder and asked, "Who owns the Mullins ranch now?"

"That so called King, I guess. Nobody has seen Mullins since Gator and his low life bunch showed up around here. Everbody just thought Mullins sold out and left the country. But dad gum it, he had one hell of a lot of friends he didn't tell nothing about it. The way things are adding up, I'd say Gator and his bunch just wiped him and his hands out. Someday we'll find their bones."

Shorty started to say something, but held off when he saw a rider slowly loping their way. "Dean, who do suppose that rider is? He sure don't seem to be in a hurry."

"Yeah, it ain't no he, and she ain't in no hurry. That's Doc Gordon's wife. Man-o-man, but she is one good-looking hide. I'd snort her flanks about anytime. But... it's a wonder she don't drown. Around men, she has her nose so high in the air, she can't be outside in the rain."

The three men stood beside their horses, waiting for her to ride up. "Hello, Dean. I saw you riding hell bent for leather, and thought I'd follow you. And... who are these gentlemen?"

Removing his hat, Dean stammered out, "This here is U.S. Marshal, Shorty Thompson, and his deputy, Buffalo. And I was riding to catch them. Why would you be interested in where I'm riding? You never follered me before."

"Oh, I just didn't have anything to do this afternoon, and thought I'd ride farther from town, this time." She turned her eyes to Shorty, as she smiled right big.

"You sure are young, and mighty good-looking to be a U.S. Marshal. Are all the Marshals as handsome as you?"

Shorty blushed a bit, and answered, "Don't know ma'am, never saw a U.S. Marshal, 'cept a couple, and myself."

Rebecca straightened in the saddle, saying, "Well Marshal, when you're back in Tascosa, please stop by for supper. Doctor Gordon is quite the cook."

She reined her horse west, and rode off in a gallop. All three men watched her rump bounce up and down, until she was completely out of sight.

Buffalo was the first to speak. "Damn, she ain't nothing but a kid! I'd say no more than twenty-five, if that. How in the hell did she wind up married to a sixty something year-old doctor? "

Dean smiled, "Buffalo, you ought'a see her step out of that saddle, with them tight riding britches on. Hell, I'm already married, and I'd damn near leave my wife just to bed that girl down a time or two. When she came to Tascosa, she had a bad rib, at least that's what was told, and she went to Doc Gordon for help. Shit, two weeks later, she was his wife. Now, old Doc Gordon has a daughter, that don't like it one bit. But what the hell, schoolteachers can be that way. To beat that, she don't do a damned thing, except look pretty. Between that stuck up, snotty daughter, and wife, Doc Gordon got the short end of the deal. He even has to do all the cooking and housekeeping. I think Doc is sorry he ever married Rebecca."

Shorty looked at Dean and asked, "Why would you think he was sorry for marrying a looker like that?"

"It shows in his eyes and face, every time she rides off by herself, for hours. It worries the hell out of him.

"And, him getting married sure has caused a rift between him and his daughter. I think Doc would just up and leave Rebecca here, if he could get his daughter to pack up and go back home with him. I just don't know for sure, but I think that good looking daughter might be getting her flanks snorted by that new lawyer that came to town a few months back. 'Bout the same time as Rebecca. Now, if that's so, Doc ain't gonna get her to budge. Killings or no killings, school or not, she won't leave."

Shorty knew there wasn't a thing he could

coming nigh on to sundown. We'd better start looking for a campsite. I'd hate to ride off in one of these dry arroyos after dark."

Dean looked toward the lowering sun, then back east. "It's only a half hours ride to the Spider Box. They will be more than glad to put us up for the night. And... you know what, it'd be a bitch if we got shot riding up there in the dark. We still got time, but we'd better kick these horses out a bit."

Riding up to the Spider Box wasn't too hard, until they got to within two hundred yards of the barns. Three quick shots vibrated the stillness of the evening. A loud voice boomed out, "Them there was warning shots! The next ones lable to hit meat! Who in the hell are you, and what do you want?"

"Damnit all to hell, Emmett! It's still light enough for you to see it's me, Dean Bessmer, and a couple of U.S. Marshals!"

"Oh, yeah, guess that is you. Sorry, but there was too much sunlight coming from behind you. Ride on in."

Riding up beside Emmett, Shorty looked into a face that a horse could stumble into any of the wrinkles. He looked to be in his eighties, with a full head of hair and five teeth in the front of his mouth. Spiting a half-cup of tobacco juice at a tumblebug, Emmett looked up at the men and grinned. "Howdy, fellers. Can't see was y'all. Jest thought I'd let you know, I see'd you. One of the boys what was in Tascosa rode in an' said y'all was coming. Over yonder's the water trough, and Dean knows where the feed is. If yer want'n to take care of yer horses, first, that is."

"Much obliged, Emmett. See you at supper."

Several cowboys were unsaddling horses, and said their howdy to Shorty, Buffalo and Dean. One of the men threw his saddle over a stall divider and slapped his horse on the rump to get him to move over. "Marshal, are y'all here for the war, or are you going to high tail it when the shooting starts?"

"Who says there is going to be a war?" Shorty threw Dunnie a half-gallon of grain, then walked to the front of the stall.

"'Spect everybody 'cept you and that dumb assed ranger what was here earlier."

"Whoa, whoa, wait a damn minute! I was told no rangers was coming to help on this one. That's why President Hayes sent me and my deputy. Matter of fact, Doc Gordon told me the same thing earlier this afternoon."

"Well, old Doc was misinformed on that one. I saw the fat ass-hole ranger myself. Rode in here like he was somebody important, and just had to talk to the boss, right away. After he half fell off his horse, I took him to see Dave."

Shorty watched the man's face, waiting for

him to say something else. When that didn't happen, Shorty asked, "and… who might Dave be?"

The man had started to walk off, but stopped and said, "He's the owner of the Spider Box, Mr. David Snyder. He's up to the main house. He don't eat in the cook shack. You gotta see him?" "Yeah, 'spect I'd better. Doc Gordon told me his name. Thanks for telling me about this ranger, it might help." Shorty dusted off his pants with his hat, as he headed for the house.

Dean hollered after him, "See you later, at the cook shack or bunkhouse, all right Shorty?"

"Oh, yeah, yeah, you and Buffalo go on and eat. I'll catch up later. I'll ask Dave where I eat and sleep."

Shorty stepped upon the porch, but before he could knock on the door, a very pretty young lady rushed out and almost knocked him over. "Oh, excuse me Ma'am! I didn't see you coming. Are you all right?"

"Yes, yes, I'm fine. Are you one of the new hired hands?"

Shorty removed his hat. "No Ma'am, I'm Shorty Thompson.

I'm the U.S. Marshal, sent here to investigate these murders and cattle rustlings. Are you Mrs. Snyder?"

She smiled a very pretty smile, and cocked her head to one side, flirting. "My goodness no!

I'm Miss Snyder. And... you look no older than me. Are you kidding about being a Marshal?"

"No Ma'am, I'm not kidding...

"Okay, okay, truce. You call my Raynell, not Ma'am or Miss Snyder, and I won't call you Marshal. I'll call you Shorty."

Shorty smiled. "That's a deal, Raynell. Now, is your father in? That's who I've come to see."

"Shucks! I mean, yes, just a moment, and I'll call him. But first, are you staying awhile? And you're not married, are you?"

"Yes, I'm staying around the country until this mess is over, and no, I'm not married."

She giggled, and then stepped back inside, calling her father. "Dad! Oh Dad! A U.S. Marshal is here to see you!"

David Snyder was a large man, almost filling the doorway as he stepped to the porch. "All Right, so you're a U.S. Marshal! If you came to tell me the same thing that smart-aleck, asshole ranger did, you can save us both some trouble by getting the hell on your horse and riding the hell out of here! Plum off my land! Do you hear me? Plum gone to hell and back!"

Raynell and Shorty both were standing with their mouths open. Before Shorty could speak, Raynell screamed, "Daddy!" She stormed into the house, slamming the door behind her.

Shorty still had his hat in his hand. "First off Mr. Snyder, I don't know what you're so pissed off at. I ain't going to tell you what to do, or not to do. I was on my way to Johnson's, when Dean Bessmer caught up to me and my deputy. Dean said you wouldn't mind us staying the night here. If that's going to be a problem, we'll be on our way. But first, I'd like to hear about the ranger that was here. I was told none was coming. That's why the President sent me, to see if I could do something. But, every where I turn, I'm running into a lot of hell from everybody."

"Dean Bessmer! He's here?" Snyder looked over Shorty.

"Yeah, he's here, down at the cookhouse." Shorty put his hat back on, not knowing whether to leave or stand there.

Snyder walked to the door and hollered inside, "Raynell, Raynell! I want you to go to the cook-shack and fetch Dean up here. And why didn't you tell me he's the one what brought the marshal? Like to have caused me to make a fool out of myself, is about what it went an' done. Oh, and you may's well have the marshal's deputy come along with Dean. We all need to do some talking. Yeah, serious talking is what we gotta do."

Raynell zipped past them in a run, but did slow down long enough to give her dad a sharp look. "Drinking, you mean!"

"Now girl! Watch yore mouth! Come on in Marshal. Come on in the house. We'll have ourselves a little snort from the bottle, while we're waiting on Dean. Matter of fact, we might have ourselves two snorts."

"Oh hell yes, I do need a drink!" Shorty removed his hat.

"Babe, oh Babe." Dave hollered to his wife. "We have company. Will you bring a bottle and several glasses?"

The glasses were goblets, and when Dave asked Shorty how much, Shorty's eyes bugged out. "My God, only a half inch in the bottom of that will last me for several days!"

A knock on the door, and Mrs. Snyder went to answer it. "Hello, Dean, and…"

Dean had his hat in his hand, saying, "Ma'am, this here is Buffalo. Deputy U.S. Marshal."

Mrs. Snyder held the door open. "Y'all come on in. Dave and the Marshal are in the pallor. Oh, Dean, didn't Raynell go fetch y'all? Didn't she come back with y'all?"

"Yes Ma'am, she fetched us, and no Ma'am, she didn't come back. I think she stayed to talk with Nathan."

Mrs. Snyder removed her apron, placing it on a rack beside the front door. Talking to herself, she hurried off the porch, headed for the barns. "That girl is looking for trouble, and will find it with that worthless, Nathan! I'll put a stop to this right now, even if I have to kill him!"

Hurrying, she saw the lantern light as it was turned low. Slowly slipping thru the barn door, she heard Raynell cooing as Nathan slipped his hand into her unbuttoned britches. Nathan went limp, covering Raynell's body. He had been hit in the back of the head with a pitchfork handle. Mrs. Snyder grabbed him by a leg and yanked him off Raynell, as her eyes flew open.

"My God Mother! What have you done?"

"Busted his skull, I hope! If you hadn't been under him, I'd have run those tines plumb thru him! Now get your shirt on and your pants pulled up and buttoned! You've got supper to fix!"

Raynell slipped her shirt around her shoulders, while looking down at the still body of Nathan. Boy, but what he had been doing to her, sure felt good. Tucking her shirttail in, and buttoning her britches, she ask, "Mama, why did you knock him out? I've never felt so good."

"Raynell, has that rotten piece of dog crap been all the way with you? Now don't lie to me, has he?"

"No, Mama, nobody has, but tonight he could have. I sure needed something. I've never felt that way before about nothing. I was about to pass out, I think. Yes, I would have fainted."

Walking back toward the house, Mrs. Snyder put her arm around Raynell. "Honey, I sure wish you'd wait for that kind of thing, but I can guess you won't. But honey, please don't let it be that little shit. He'll be on and off before you even know he was on. You'll be left flustered, and wondering why there wasn't more. Get yourself a real man for your first try. Then you'll know true satisfaction. That little shit would leave you to take care of yourself. That's enough to make a woman mad at all men."

As they got to the porch, Raynell ask, "Mama, why do you call Nathan, little? After all, he's over six feet tall."

"Honey, I'm talking little where big counts."

"Mama, are you saying what I think you're saying? Nathan has had you! Oh my God, when?"

"It was last spring, when your papa went on that five month cattle drive. Anyway, it was mating season for all the animals. You know, the studs and mares, the bulls and cows. Mating was just in the air. Nathan walked in on me while I was taking my bath, and I let things get out of hand. Honey, I'm telling you, that man couldn't satisfy a she goat. He had his pants back on and was gone before I even had my legs spread completely apart. Don't let it be him, you'll die, or either want to kill him."

Raynell reached and kissed her mother on the cheek. "Thanks Mama. I promise, I'll let it be a man. But mama, darn I wish he was still doing it, or at least finished, just this one time. If you'd have been three minutes later, something would have happened. I could feel it. I was about to explode. And... I'm sure I'd have liked it. But you're right, later it'll happen with a man. Lets get supper on the table. I'll bet everyone is starved."

Shorty and Dean had told David the word was about that Jack Johnson and his men wouldn't make it to Tascosa. David took another large drink from his glass before saying, "Yeah, I also heard that, but by damned they'll make it if I've got anything to say about it. Come morning, we'll take as many men as this place can spare, and go meet them. After that, we'll all ride into Tascosa together. After supper, we're gonna hit the hay pretty damned quick, then be on the trail right after breakfast in the morning. It'll be good and light by then, so we won't be ambushed by that Chinaman and his outfit."

Shorty stood to leave, but asked, "Dave, do you have any idea where the outlaws might try and hit Jack and his men?"

"Yeah, my guess would be around Buzzard Gap. The river cuts thru a low hill and is only about a hundred yards wide at that point. And again, our rains ain't come yet, so the water is no more than knee deep on a horse, and a hundred and fifty feet wide."

"How far to this Buzzard Gap?" Shorty was moving toward the door, with Dean, and Buffalo already holding it open.

Dave took one more drink saying, "It's about half way between here and Johnson's spread. We can make it in four, maybe five hours at the most. We ought'a meet up with Jack pretty close to there. Least wise that's what I'm hoping."

"All right, we'll see you after breakfast. We'll all hit the sack early." Shorty put his hat on as he stepped to the porch.

"Buffalo, what do you think of heading back into Tascosa in the morning, just to see if you can learn anything?"

"Shorty, I'd sure like to go along with y'all. Just in case Booger and Gator show up to hit Johnson. I'd like to be there."

"Yeah, your right. Lets get some sleep."

Breakfast in the cook shack was extra noisy, as everyone was wondering who Dave was taking with him and who would be left behind to guard the ranch. Nathan finished with his food first and got up from the table. "Well, I can't go along this morning. My horse threw a shoe yesterday afternoon, and Smitty is going to put some new ones on. That'll take most of the morning."

For saying that, he received a couple of dirty looks and a yeah, yeah, we know. "Afraid of getting yer ass shot off?"

Nathan blowed up and started cussing. "Now y'all know damn well better than that! Sides that somebody has to stay here in case we need to defend the ranch! I'll just be one of them!" He stormed out, slamming the door behind him.

Breakfast was finished and all the coffee gone, before the men headed for the corral to rope and saddle their horses. Shorty, Dean and Buffalo were waiting for Dave to show up, when Raynell came down the trail toward them. Dean smiled, saying, "Boy, before long that girl is going to be a hand full for some ole boy. She can ride and rope about as well as any hand on this ranch. Nathan has been trying to snort her flanks for about a month now. If Mrs. Snyder finds out about it she'll cut his balls off an' stick em' in his mouth. She don't like that boy one damn bit. Probably has good reason. He's about as sorry as they come."

Raynell was all smiles as she asked Dean, "Have you seen Nathan this morning? I've got something to tell him."

"Yeah, he's over at the blacksmith's. He's having new shoes put on his horse today. Guess he's staying here."

"No he ain't! Daddy said!"

Dave walked up, overhearing Raynell talk. "Daddy said what? What are you getting me into now?" Dave had his hands on his hips, and a grin on his face.

"Nothing, I ain't getting you into nothing. I just said Nathan wadn't staying here today. That's all."

"Well you'd better scoot yourself on back up to the house. Your mama is needing yore help with the dishes. And try to stay out of trouble today while I'm gone."

"Yes daddy, I never get into trouble. Bye fellers, all y'all be careful. See you when you get back. Just wish I could go along."

Turning to Shorty, Dave cleared his throat. Sorry I'm a little late. I figgered I'd best write some things down for my wife. You know, just in case I don't come back. I could get shot."

While Dave saddled his horse, Shorty was asking some questions. "About how long have you and Johnson been here?"

"Nigh on to fifteen years. When we came out here to the Panhandle, wadn't nothing but Indians and a few Buffalo. When we first came, we built ourselves a couple of half dugouts to live in. Wadn't too long before the Indians figgered out they couldn't burn us out, so we became friends with the most of 'em. Hell, when we'd have a bad winter, I'd give them a few head of beef to hold them over. Next spring they'd show up here with twenty-five or thirty head of unbranded longhorns. Said they picked them up below the Red River. My guess is they was a bunch of strays from cattle drives. Most of the Indians have now moved on over into the strip. Well, we'd better ride. We've got a ways to go."

Turning to his men, he told which ones were going and who was to stay and guard the ranch. "Ben, you and Fred spread the men out

so every trail is guarded. I don't want to come
back here and find I've been burnt out. Keep
a sharp eye. Oh, and tell Nate to catch up with
us when Smitty is done with his horse."

CHAPTER FIVE

Dave waved his hat in the air, and everyone mounted, riding off toward the east. Including Shorty, Dean and Buffalo, thirty-seven men, with their horses in a long, slow lope, were leaving a dust trail close to a hundred feet into the sky. The men riding farther back, swung wide to stay out of the dust. Everyone was thankful they didn't have a west wind to contend with, but could have used a breeze from the south. The morning air was very still, and unmoving, and the temperature was rising.

An hour into the ride the men started talking, talking loud enough to be heard over the pounding hoof beats. "Dave, what brings an area together to fight a stronger force, knowing they are going to lose several friends and neighbors? And a few damn good hands?" Shorty had been thinking of how many men they must face in the coming showdown.

"Shorty, us ranchers and farmers are building the west. The farmers grow feed for our cattle when we have bad winters. Also they grind wheat into flour, and corn into cornmeal to feed us. In turn us ranchers sell or trade them beef. And we ship our cattle to market back east to feed the nation. I reckon we'll always have some crooked ass hole that wants to take everything for themselves, and what they can't take they'll try to destroy. But Shorty, we've made up our minds, we'll die before we lose what we've got here. It's too damned important to these United States of America. We will build the west, and make a fair living doing it. We may have to kill a few underhanded bastards to get it done, and we will if we have to."

Dave half stood in his saddle, turning his head to check on the men coming behind them. "Shorty, them clouds to the northwest shor are building early. They keep building and we could get us a much-needed shower this afternoon. We're lable to get our asses wet 'fore we get back home. Well let's hook 'em, we ought'a be at Buzzards gap in less than an hour. Guess we ought'a drop off here and water ourselves and the horses. Then we'll pull back up here to the south bank. I don't want to get caught in that river bottom. Don't want'a be hit by Gator and his men, or a flash flood. No telling what it could be."

As the horses lowered their heads to drink from the clear, slow moving water, cowboys filled their canteens. Shorty looked to the next bend in the river. "Dave, how come that place is called Buzzard Gap? Kind'a strange name for a water gap."

Dave stood from filling his canteen, and pushed the cork back into the opening.

"It was fourteen years ago this month. There was a hell of a good-sized wagon train on its way to the Salt River Valley in Arizona. They had upwards of a thousand head of cattle and several hundred head of horses. Anyway when they got to the river, instead of spending the night on the north side, they decided to forge the river in the dim darkness of the evening.

"Nobody in his right mind would have tried that. You don't forge a unknown river at night. There had been lightening for several hours far up river to the northwest. Matter of fact, the clouds looked a bunch like them that's over that way right now.

Anyway, as the people, wagons, horses and cattle started across, a flash flood hit 'em hard and swept them down river, slamming them against those bluffs at the bottom of the next gap. Less than half the animals, and only fifty-one of the three hundred or so people survived. For the next month, buzzards by the thousands came to feed on the decaying carcasses. Hell their circle was more than a mile high, and looked like a black cyclone. We could see them all the way from my place. So, that is why it's called Buzzards Gap."

Horses dug in their hoofs, pulling themselves up the south bank of the river. Turning east again, Dave kept his horse to a walk. "No need in rushing the rest of the way. We'll be there in less than half an hour. We ought'a be meeting up with Jack and his bunch about any time now."

Turning in the saddle, and looking over his shoulder, Dave gave out a shrill whistle. Waving his hat, he called for two men to come on up front. "Rod, you and Dinger ride on toward the river bank and keep an eye open for any of that outlaw bunch. If you see anything, wave your hat, and don't fire your gun unless you're shot at. Now be careful and don't get your balls in a bind."

Shorty was looking to the north, while standing tall in the stirrups. "Hey Dave, have you noticed that cloud of dust over there? Looks to be a couple of miles, maybe more."

Everyone stopped their horses and looked to where Shorty was pointing. Dean spoke up. "Too far for us to tell what it is from here. Looks to be heading due west. Could be a herd of antelope, or even wild horses. Why don't me and Buffalo ride over that'a way and have ourselves a look-see? Could even be Gator and that bunch. We'll find out then meet up again with y'all on your way back by here. Shouldn't take us more'n an hour."

Dave looked at Shorty, who nodded his

head. "Let me get my field glasses out of my saddle-bag. Maybe I can save you a trip." Shorty lifted the glasses to his eyes.

I'd say that is anywhere between fifty and sixty men headed west by northwest. If I didn't know better, I'd say that brown horse out front was Nate's. His horse does have a little bit of white on one ear, don't it?" Shorty handed the glasses to Dave.

Dave studied the fast moving horses, and looked at all of the men. "Too far to tell, but I don't think so. That horse looks too small, and 'sides that, Nate's back at the ranch, having shoes put on his horse. Dean, you and Buffalo go ahead and see what you can, but watch you're asses. No telling who that is. Hope the hell it ain't Johnson's bunch."

As Dean and Buffalo headed for the river, Shorty asked Dave, "You don't suppose that really could be Gator and his bunch, do you? Like maybe been here and gone. I'd hate for Buffalo and Dean to run into that gang by their selves. Dean said their hideout hole was north of the river a few miles."

"Yeah, it is, but it's back closer to New Mexico. They're a good ten or twelve miles west by northwest of Tasacosa, at the old Mullens place."

Twenty minutes later, Buzzard Gap was seen just a little north of due east. Jack Johnson and his men were nowhere in sight. "Shorty, what time does your watch say? By the sun, it's nigh on to ten, maybe even ten-thirty." Dave wiped sweat from his brow, as he stood in the stirrups, and strained his eyes.

Shorty pulled his watch from his vest pocket. "It's ten till eleven. Hadn't we ought'a met up with Jack before now?"

"Yeah, lets head on over to the gap, and wait there for a little while. Ain't like Jack being late. None a'tall. Hope the hell that wasn't Gator's bunch, and they already hit Jack and his men."

Shorty lifted one leg around the saddle horn, resting. "Did anybody tell Jack y'all was going meet him here?"

"Well, no, but word was about that he was coming in today, so we could figger out how to get that Chinaman's bunch."

Just shy of noon, Dave told his men to dowse their coffee fire, and get ready to ride. "Shorty, I sure don't like it, Jack not showing up 'fore now. Maybe Gator and his fellers got word somehow that we was all coming here. Hell, maybe they went and hit Jack at his place. We'd better ride on over that'a way and see." Dave thought a minute then hollered at a couple of his men.

"Glen, you and Stinker come on over here for a minute."

Both men dropped the bridle reins to the ground, and emptied their coffee cups on the dying coals of their fire. Glen was the first to speak. "Yes Sir, Mister Snyder, what'da ya need?"

"Glen, when y'all went to Tascosa the other week end, did y'all let anybody know we was coming out here to the gap to meet up with Johnson's bunch?"

"Now you know better than that, Mister Snyder. We don't talk about what or when yer going to do anything. We don't talk yore affairs over with nobody."

"Naw, naw, Glen. I wadn't saying you was on purpose opening yore mouth. I meant like getting drunk and blabbing to some whore." Dave did not miss trust his men.

"Sir, we didn't get drunk that Saturday. We just went in for a couple of beers and a woman. Had 'em both and came home."

"Well Glen, you check with everybody that went to town that day, and see of they might have let anything slip to one of them whores. If they did, we need to know which one it was and stop it. There are more than enough spies in that damn place."

A shrill whistle from one of the men got everyone's attention. "Riders coming, Mister Snyder! Looks to be at least forty, maybe even fifty of 'em coming from the east. Couldn't tell if it's Johnson's outfit or not. They're still a bit too far off."

Everyone looked to the east, as Shorty

reached for his field glasses. "Here, Dave, look through these."

"Yep, it's Johnson all right. Looks as if he's got his self a couple of prisoners. Thrust up like two turkey's, and bloody."

A young cowboy called Jeepers, asked, "Mister Snyder, you mean by looking through that thing, you can tell all that?"

"Shor 'nuff, Jeeper. Take a look." Dave handed the glasses.

"My God!! It's like they was already here! I can even see the tobacco stains on Lum's chin! There, he just spit a gob, right then! I never knowed they was anything in the whole world like these here things! Glory be, won't nobody believe me, when I tell 'em what I saw! Nobody a'tall. How far off would you say they are right now?" Jeeper handed the field glasses to Shorty. "Don't matter if they believe me or not. I know what I saw, and nobody can ever take that away from me. Not ever." He smiled, quietly.

"Nigh on to three quarters of a mile, would be my guess." Shorty brought the glasses to his eyes, as Dave's men began to dismount, waiting for Johnson's bunch to ride up. Some leaned against their horse, while others just sat on their heels and rolled a smoke, or took a chew of tobacco.

Jack Johnson's face was stern, as he and his men rode within talking distance of Shorty and

Dave. Dave raised his voice, shouting to Jack.

"Well I can guess these two fellers is why you're late! Knowed it had to be something! What's it about?"

Jack and his men dismounted, jerking two badly beaten men to the ground. Jack removed his hat and using his shirtsleeve, wiped his face and forehead dry of sweat. "Dave, we stopped off at my northwest line camp to pick up my brother-in-law, Bruce. When we got there we found Bruce dead about half way between the barn and house. The other two boys was found in the coral where it looks like they was fixin' to saddle their horses. We looked the place over for my sister, Darline, but she was nowhere about. Wouldn't be like her to run off after Bruce being shot."

Dave cut in and interrupted Jack. "Where'd you get these two fellers? Looks to me like they've been worked over."

"Well, after burying Bruce, we'd headed on over this'a way, and you remember that water spring bog about a quarter mile south of the second river bend?"

"Yeah, that's where you lose a head of beef or so a year."

"Well we rode slowly up to that and found one of these fellers still on his horse, and belly deep in that bog. The other feller there was laying on top of Darline, raping her. He was paying no mind to his partner that was screaming his head off and slowly sinking out of sight. Anyway, we got 'em and I sent a couple of boys back to my place with Darline. Told 'em to bypass the line camp."

None of the men had spoken a word; they just glared at the two bruised, bloody men. Hanging was on their minds.

"Jack, no words can tell you how sorry I am to have heard that. How is Darline taking it?" Dave shared everyone's sorrow.

"Hell, she's fine. Who did you think give these bastards their bloody, bruised bodies? It was her! Man, when we pulled that polecat off her, she bounced up and kicked him right in the balls. Hell, she whopped up on him for a good ten minutes before she realized she was still naked. While she put her clothes on, we pulled the other one out of the bog. No more'n did we get that done, when she jumped on him before we could hold her off. She used that same piss elm'um club that she'd used on the other one. She had that worthless bastard out cold in no more than three or four good blows. You know, for a kid that weights no more than a sack of grain, that sis of mine can get mean'ern a sick dog."

Shorty walked over and stuck out his hand. I'm Shorty Thompson, U S Marshal."

"The hell you say! Well you're damn neigh too late! We're taking care of that Chinaman and his bunch before sundown tomorrow.

We're cleaning out the whole damn bunch!"

"Care if ask what you have planned for these two?" Shorty was surprised that either of them was still alive.

"Taking them to the law in Tascosa! We'll more'n likely have to change the law when we get there, but that can be done before he can blow his nose twice. These polecats are going to hang, legal like. A judge will do it, or I will!"

Dave almost had a barn kicking fit. "What in the hell are you talking about, Jack? What law? Law my ass! You know that bastard is on that Chinaman's payroll! They'll be turned loose 'fore you walk across the street to the saloon!"

"Naw, these two already know, if I see them anywhere except behind bars, they're dead. And they can't run far, or fast enough to hide. I'll send men after them, no matter where they go. They been told they'll be drug behind a horse 'til they ain't got no hide left, then they're to be hung on the spot."

Dave smiled, "Well we know where they'll stay tonight; locked in my storm cellar. We can still make it to my place before dark. Then in the morning we'll all ride into Tascosa.

Everyone was unsaddling and rubbing down horses when Raynell came running up. "How'd it go, Dad? Don't see any blood or bullet holes on no body. I see nobody is missing 'cept Nate. Didn't he come back with y'all?"

"Everything went along all right. Nate never showed up. What time did he leave here noway? Oh, just a minute." Dave turned to his men.

"Glen, you and Wilford make sure these two are locked in the cellar and fed and watered. I want a guard kept on that door tonight. Now what was I saying? Oh yeah, Nate leaving here?"

Raynell was making eyes at Shorty and almost didn't hear her dad asking a question. "I don't know, Dad, I was helping Mother. I just saw Smitty was working on the windmill and not putting shoes on no horse. Ask him, he'll know."

A frown moved across Dave's face, but he said nothing. After rubbing his horse down and throwing him a half-gallon of grain, he headed for the blacksmith shop. Over his shoulder, he hollered at the men. "Shorty, Jack, y'all and the boys go on to the cook shack. I'll be along dreckly."

Smitty looked from his work, as Dave walked in. "Smitty, what in the hell are you doing in here, working this late?"

"Early this morning I noticed some slop in one of the windmill sucker rods. Figgered I'd better get it fixed 'fore it broke plum' loose. Just got it done. How'd it go today?"

"Not bad, not bad. Say, what time did you get done with Nate's horse? He never showed up."

"I never touched his horse. After y'all rode out, he said maybe he'd better wait on them shoes. But a funny thing, when he rode off after y'all, he kicked the hell out of his horse, turning north after riding only a mile 'er so east. I saw him turn when I was on top of the windmill. He was using his quirt on that horse's butt harder than a man ought'a. Animals don't need to be beat."

"Well, heading north shor's hell ain't no short-cut towards Johnson's place. I think Nates in trouble, next time I see him. I don't like to be double-crossed by nobody, specially by a hired hand." Dave was very upset.

"Want me to get our tracker to go take a look as to where he went? You don't suppose he's one of them there spies, do you?"

Smitty knew how Dave was feeling. A hired hand selling out to the enemy just ain't done. You rode for the brand, or you didn't ride at all. No, maybe they was wrong and when Nate returned, if he returned, it could all be explained. Well, maybe.

"Naw, it's too close to dark. We'll hold off and maybe he'll come back in a day er two. Hell, anything could have happened."

CHAPTER SIX

Town folk stood in their doorways, in vacant lots and on wooden walkways watching well over seventy men ride into Tascosa. Jack Johnson raised his hand for all the riders to stop. The street was full of horses and men as they dismounted in front of the small, rock jailhouse. As the two killers were jerked from their horses, a deputy came running up and ask, "What y'all doing with Jeb and Ned? Y'all know that they're deputy Texas Rangers, don't you?" Why'er they all tied up? Sheriff Keefer ain't gonna like that one bit! I'm gonna go get him right now! And I know Texas Ranger Norman will have a fit."

As all the men found hitching space for their horses and dismounted, the deputy headed across the street to the saloon.

Shorty just had to ask, "Jack, who and what in the hell was that? Acted like a snot-nosed, tattle-tail kid."

Jack grinned, "Yeah, that's about what he is. He's a harmless little shit. Just playing big shot with that deputy badge. I'm afraid that the dumb assed sheriff is going to get him killed."

Jack, Dave and Shorty had the two bound men on the walkway as Sheriff Keefer came pushing his way through the crowd. "Jack Johnson, just what in the hell do you think you're doing? You can't hog-tie two deputy Texas Rangers and...!"

Jack had him by the shirtfront and jerked him damn near off his feet. "Listen you dumb, worthless ass hole! These men are going to be held in jail for murder! They will stay in jail until the Judge gets here, even if that's a year from now!"

Sheriff Keefer grabbed his hat, setting it back on his head. "We'll just see about that, Mister big shot! You ranchers can't push yer way in here and think yer going to run my town!"

Pushing his way through laughing men, Keefer headed back for the saloon. Five minutes later he was standing in the jailhouse door, with a four hundred pound, five foot nine inch mouth behind him. "Now Mister big shot rancher, Jack Johnson! You give me them cell keys and get the hell out of my jail! This man is Texas Ranger, Raymond Wendal Norman! Those are his deputies you have locked up in my jail!" Keefer tried to talk with authority, but had a quiver in his voice and was as pale as a sick kid.

Shorty stepped forward. "Ranger Norman,

how is it that I got a wire from the President of these United States, saying the Texas Rangers couldn't give these people any help, so he sent me. But now, not only is there a Texas Ranger here, but he also has his self two deputies. Oh, I forgot to introduce myself. I'm U.S. Marshal M D Thompson, and I also have myself deputy, called Buffalo. He'll be around later, he's chasing a dust cloud."

"He's What? Never mind, Marshal, being as Texas did send me, I'll handle things from here on, and certainly don't need your help! You and your deputy are relieved of all responsibility of this case! From here on out, I am the law in these parts."

Shorty just stood there, smiling. "Mister Norman, you seem to be about as full of shit as this town sheriff. Nobody but the President tells me what to do or what not to do. I am still on his payroll and this case! Now, what in the hell were your men doing out on the Johnson spread? Why did they kill Bruce Bass?"

"I had no idea my men had killed anyone. They had papers to arrest Mister Bass and bring him in to be questioned. We have information that several of the surrounding ranchers are about to take the law into their own hands and do harm to a fellow rancher. I was sent here to see that doesn't happen. Now, if my deputies had to kill that man, I would say he resisted arrest and was about to harm officers of the law. You will free them immediately!".

"Naw, naw, we can't do that. You see, they will stay right here in this jail until the judge shows up, whenever that is."

Sheriff Keefer mouthed off again. "You see here now! You can't just come in here and take over my jail! I am the duly appointed Sheriff of Tascosa, and wil…"

He never got to finish what he was saying. David Snyder had him a foot in the air by his shirtfront. "You suck egg dog! Nobody in this town appointed you to nothing! That fat Chinaman, Gator, and Booger threatened the town council into doing it! So don't get smart with us, or you'll be right back there in one of those cells with them other ass holes!"

Sheriff Keefer caught Ranger Norman by the shirtsleeve, saying, "Come on Ranger, Judge Wingate will be here before the end of the week! He'll give warrants for every lasting one of these law breakers!" Turning, they headed back for the saloon.

Once they were in the street, Ranger Norman changed directions and headed for the livery. Keefer had taken several steps, and was talking to himself, before he noticed he was alone.

"Reyes, 'er Norman, where in the hell are you going? We need to plan and do some talking! Now, dammit, now!"

PAUL L. THOMPSON

Norman stopped and turned, facing Keefer. "Keefer, I'm getting the hell out of here, and let Gator and Booger handle this! If you had one damn brain cell in your head, you'd do the same thing! That little bastard in there is a real U.S. Marshal! Nobody told me a U. S. Marshal was going to be in on this!"

"Well go ahead and run you coward! If I'd known you had no guts, I'd have gotten somebody else to be Ranger Norman! When Judge Wingate gets here, you'll see! We own him lock stock and barrel. I am the town Sheriff!"

Keefer turned on his heels and hurried for the lawyer's office. "Mister Farren, a couple of the men got caught and hauled to jail. You know, the ones we sent to Johnson's spread to kill that Bass family. You've got to get them out so they won't talk."

"How in the hell did they get caught? Can't any of these idiots follow instructions? They were to kill Bass and his wife and the other two men that were there. Then all they had to do was burn the damn place to the ground! If we're going to own this country, we have got to put the fear of God into these idiots! Come on, I'll get them out on bond, then they can head out to Gator and Jun Dung."

"Well, the way they got caught is, instead of killing the woman, they took her with them and raped her. Ned was still mounted on her when Johnson and his men showed up.

"Oh, Reyes, 'er Norman has already headed for Jun Dung."

"He What? That stupid, fat bastard will get shot! He can't be going out there! People will know he's tied in with Gator, and that could blow this whole deal sky high!"

Four of Jacks men were guarding the two men in jail. "What do you mean there is no bail? Don't just stand here, go get that Marshal, and have him here in two minutes flat!" Farren was running a good bluff, at least on Jack's men.

Jack looked up as his man came through the saloon door. Sliding back his chair, in two strides he was at his man's side. "What happened? Somebody try to bust 'em out?"

"Naw, but that lawyer, Farren is over there hotter'n hell. He wants them two released on bail. Wants to talk to Shorty, now."

"Go back over there and tell him I said go to hell. They're staying put. If he tries anything, shoot him!"

Shorty had walked up and over heard what was said. "Shoot who?" He looked from Jack to James.

"Farren! He's an idiot lawyer and wants them two out on bond. It ain't gonna happen." Jack started back to his table.

"Hold on a minute, Jack. Maybe I ought'a go talk with him. He could cause us a problem with the judge."

"Shorty, he's a smart little shit head that showed up here several months ago and gets every one of them bastards off that has ever been arrested. He showed up a couple of months before Sheriff Bone went and got killed. Then that damn Keefer was put in Sheriff Bone's place, and not one robber, killer, rustler or no body else has been convicted of nothing since. No, he's bought and paid for just like the sheriff."

"Makes no difference, Jack. Everybody in entitled to consul and a fair trial. That's the law. I'll go talk with him."

Shorty was surprised when he met Farren. "Mister Farren, I'm M D Thompson, U.S. Marshal. You wanted to talk?"

"Yes, Marshal. I want these men released on bail, immediately! Why was I not called upon when they were incarcerated? That is a violation of the law!"

Shorty looked at him for a long minute. "Mister Farren, you're full of shit. The only law that has been broken is them two worthless pieces of dog shit killing a man and raping his wife! Now, when the judge gets here, if he sees fit to let them two out on bail that is up to him and would be on his shoulders when they run! I have no idea who is paying you to defend those two, but I hope it's a bunch, 'cause if I have anything to do with it, they'll hang! Now it'd be best if you went on about your other business and not get shot by one of these men guarding this jail."

Farren sputtered and sucked air. "Marshal, evidently you have no idea who you are dealing with! I am Oliver Farren the third! My grandfather and father are U.S. Senators and we have law offices in three cities! I will have your job! Do I make myself clear? I will have your job!"

Shorty smiled, "Now I know you're full of shit. Nobody in his right mind would want my job. Too beat that, President Hayes appointed me U.S. Marshal. Only he can fire me and it would take a full act of congress to override the President."

"I at least want the sheriff to be in charge here."

"Can't be done. Come back when the judge shows up."

"Marshal, may I at least talk with my clients?"

"Yep, these boys will have to make sure you're not tote'n any iron. Can't have them fellers gabbin' a weapon and shooting their way out of here."

"I always carry a weapon! But here it is, for now!"

"Go ahead, you've got ten minutes."

"What do you mean, ten minutes? If you think... Forget it!"

Farren was not allowed in the cell and had

to stand in front of the cell door. "Listen, Jeb, Ned, you have nothing to worry about. Judge Wingate will be here by the end of the week and we'll have you out of here with all charges dropped. All you have to do is sit tight and keep your mouths shut. My God, did Johnson and his men beat the hell out of you? You look as if a wagon ran over you and dragged you for miles."

Ned looked and Jeb. "Well yeah, they took turns on us."

Jeb got up from the side of the bunk and put a finger through the bars. "Farren, you'd better get us the hell out of here! Where in the hell is Reyes? I mean Norman? That bastard told us we'd get into no trouble for doing his dirty work."

Farren turned red in the face. "Just keep your voice down and your mouths shut! Do you want the whole world to hear what you're saying? You don't want to insinuate you are going to talk. Gator would not like that tone in your voice. Now shut up, and we'll get you released."

Ned jumped to the bars. "Listen here you little squirt, I'll pull you through these bars and rip your damned head off! Either you or Keefer get the hell out to Gator and let him know what's going on. I don't mean next week, ass hole! Now!"

"Now you listen here, you can't talk to me

in that tone! I'll not have it! Do you hear me? Not one more word out of you!" Farren turned and stormed from the cell area.

"Marshal, when Judge Wingate arrives I'll have charges brought against Mister Johnson. His men beat the living daylights out of those men after they were bound and tied."

"You're full of shit! The Bass woman they were raping did it! There are forty witnesses to that effect."

Farren's mouth flew open as he sputtered and slammed the door closed as he was leaving.

Ned hung onto the cell bars for several minutes before speaking to his partner. "You know Jeb, when we get out of here, I'm going to kill that little bastard just to hear him squeal."

Shorty sat down across from David and Jack, and ordered himself a beer. "You fellers happen to know this Judge Wingate? That cocky little lawyer, Farren, sure will try and cause us mucho problems. He's mighty proud of his bringing ups."

All the men shook their heads yeah, they had heard of Judge Wingate. Jack took a swallow of his beer and said, "Yeah, it's the same judge that's been coming for the past several months. But Shorty, any problems will be short lived. I'll jerk those men out of that jail and take them all the way to Austin before I let some stupid judge like Wingate set them free.

Maybe it'd be safer if I just went on over there and put a couple of damn bullets in their heads. But no matter, they'll not slide on this one."

"Now Jack, you don't want to do that. If that is a crooked judge, you'd hang sure as hell, no matter why you did it."

Everyone was surprised when in walked lawyer Farren and Texas Ranger Norman. They looked odd walking together. Farren was a well dressed, good looking five foot eleven inch, one hundred and eighty pounder, while Norman was about five-seven, weighing close to four hundred, and as sloppy as if he's just gotten up from the hog trough. Norman threw out his chest as he confronted Shorty. "Marshal, the Texas Rangers will file a writ with Judge Wingate when he arrives, that will remove you from any jurisdiction in this case." Turning to Farren, he asked, "What did you call that paper? I disremember."

Farren turned red in the face. "It's called a restraining order. It removes any authority Marshal Thompson thinks he has involving those two arrested deputy rangers. The Texas Rangers have the right to appoint their deputies without the interference of any outsiders. That includes U.S. Marshals."

Jack and David looked at Shorty, who was smiling. "Ranger Norman, you and Farren had better let go of that log and swim for your life. The way I see it, you both are about to drown.

No Judge, and I do mean none at all can over ride the President. You can not have me removed from this or any other case. Now, the U.S Supreme Court probably could, but that would take years. Them two killers will already be worm food long before that."

"Mister smart aleck Marshal, come morning, we'll see!" Farren and Norman headed for the door.

"Oh Mister Farren, would you have a short moment to talk. I need some advise." Mrs. Gordon had stopped her horse in the middle of the street and waved a gloved hand at lawyer Farren.

"Yes ma'am, if that is your wish. Please come to my office in just a few minutes." Farren then turned to Ranger Norman.

"Reyes, 'er shit, Norman you go on over to my house and wait for me. Oh, I'm thankful that you changed your mind about riding out to see Jun Dung. It might have gotten you killed. Judge Wingate is suppose to stop by and stay the night at my place, and we all need to talk about this U.S. Marshal."

"Rebecca, you know never to come to my office to talk! You keep this up and the Doctor, as well as other people might start asking questions. Now, what is so important?"

"Darling, what are you going to do about that little U.S. Marshal? I certainly think he is going to be a very large problem. Should I get him interested in me, at this time?"

Farren was pacing the floor. "No, no, I don't think that will be necessary. Judge Wingate should be at my house before sundown. I'm sure he can handle that Marshal. Gator and his men have already taken care of his deputy, along with Dean Bessmer. No, Marshal Thompson just thinks he has the upper hand. This is too big of an operation for some little squirt of a U.S. Marshal to mess up. The only thing we have to worry about is Jeb and Ned. If those two start talking to the town people before we get them out of jail, and away from here, they could cause us serious problems. Now, you'd better leave."

Rebecca started to step to the walkway, but turned and closed the door. "Dear, if I catch you with that little redheaded school teacher again, I will shoot you right between the eyes. Do I make myself clear? I think you are carrying it much too far."

"What in the hell do you mean? She's Gordon's daughter, and you're married to Gordon!"

Me being married to Doctor Gordon is the job you gave me! To me it is work, putting up with that old goat! There is nothing pleasant about it! What you are doing with his daughter is strictly pleasure! It will stop immediately! Do you hear me?"

"We'll see! Just you stop bossing me

around!"

She wanted to reach over and scratch his eyes out but didn't. Her eyes were shinning as she stepped to the walkway, thanking lawyer Farren, as two men walked by. "Mister Farren, thank you for your help. I will return later with my husband, and we will sign the papers. I am sure it will all work out for the best. I'd hate to get someone else!"

The men had tipped their hats, walking down the sidewalk. Swinging into the saddle, Rebecca loped her horse down the street to the barn behind Doctor Gordon's house. She did not unsaddle, or feed and water the horse.

As she stepped into the kitchen, Doctor Gordon looked up from the stove and gave her a huge smile. "How was your ride, dear? You weren't gone as long as usual."

"It was a swell ride, darling. I'm just a bit tired. I think I'll take a short nap. Please call me when you have supper ready."

Before interring the bedroom, she called over her shoulder. "Oh dear, you'll have to unsaddle and take care of the horse, I'm just too tired. And don't forget to water her."

Doctor Gordon heard the bedroom door close as he sat down at the table with his head in his hands. "Yes dear, yes dear. Give me strength, Lord, please give me strength."

Doc had heard the same tone in her voice that had become so familiar, and he didn't like it at all. Was he coming to his senses? "Why in the world did I marry this woman forty years my junior? After all, I had only known her two weeks when we got hitched. Stupid, lonely old man, that's why! That's me! Now what am I to do? Lord, please guide me and help me through my darkest hours."

CHAPTER SEVEN

Buffalo and Dean had cut cross-country, coming in behind a large group of horsemen. They weren't riding as fast as it had looked from the other side of the river. "Buffalo, I think these fellers are Gator's men. If they are and we get caught, we're in a heap of trouble. That man has a personal hate for me."

As they traveled a few miles due north of Tascosa, a lone rider cut from the bunch and headed due south.

"You know Buffalo, that damn near looks like Nate on that horse. I just wish I'd paid more attention to what he was wearing this morning. A set of them field glasses would help right now. Boy, that white-eared horse sure reminds me of his. You don't suppose he's one of the spies, do youuuu! Oh shit, Buffalo, sit tight and don't go for your gun, we're covered. Looks like there is at least three of them that I can see, with rifles pointed right at us."

"Y'all fellers just sit tight!" A man with a rifle hanging loosely in one hand, walked from behind a scrub cedar tree. Two other men were now moving around to either side of them, while one more approached from the rear.

"Dean, what in the hell are you doing foller'n' us? You know it'll get you killed. Who's this big ox riding with you?"

"His name's Buffalo. He's a friend of mine from over near Arizona, by way of Wyoming. We're gonna head down south and see if we can pick up some strays and restock my place. You bastards only left me a few more than fifty head. Can't make a living with what's left. We was just headed back to my place now. I was going to pick up a couple more men and supplies."

"Well Dean, I think you're as full of shit as a constipated hog. But we'll see what Gator has to say about it. Let's ride."

Riding into the old Mullins ranch was more than Dean could believe, though he had seen it day before yesterday. Topping a low rise and looking into a small valley, they could see and hear several thousand head of cattle. Without looking at Buffalo, Dean whispered, "See what I meant, Buffalo. These bastards have half the cattle in west Texas, and they're all stolen. They must be getting ready to push these to the railhead in Hayes City."

"What the hell you yammering about, Dean? Best if you kept shut an' keep all your talk for Gator. He just might want to kill you this time. You was told to stop snoopin' round here."

"Damnit, I wasn't snooping around here! You threw down on us and brought us here! We was on our way to my place! Now lets get to Gator and get this over with!"

Gator was as big and ugly as Buffalo had seen every night in his dreams for two years. Everything flashed before his eyes again. The raid on the ranch by men they thought was U.S. Cavalry. It was too late when they found out it was really Gator with his gunmen wearing stolen uniforms. They fired at anything that moved. Several of the ranch hands were killed, along with a stage driver and three passengers. Tears seeped from his eyes as he again saw his beautiful wife Kathline gunned down right before his very eyes. Then he himself was shot and wounded and had to wait days to pursue the killers.

His partner, U.S. Marshal Shorty Thompson got back to the ranch, and with Buffalo, trailed Gator and Booger to San Francisco before the bastards jumped on a ship headed for China. Now, right here in front of him was one of the murdering bastards he had dreamed about and tried to find for these long two years.

Buffalo was shaken from his thoughts with a voice he hated.

"Dean, Dean, Dean. Just what in the hell am I suppose to do with you? You keep this up and I'll have to kill you, sister or no sister. It's starting to make me look bad in front of the men." For just a moment, Gator looked straight into Buffalo's eyes.

"Do I know you, big feller?

Buffalo wanted to grab him and jerk his head off. "No, Sir. Can't say as I've had the pleasure. Ever been to Wyoming?"

"Naw, naw, never that far north. Well Dean, here's what I'm gonna do, just to keep the peace with that sister of yours. I'll let Bender and Norris take y'all over that hill to the north, that's toward your place, and they'll fire off a couple of shots in the air. Y'all ride off and Bender and Norris will come back here saying they took care of you. They'll say they tied you to your horses and sent 'em on toward your place. Now Dean, don't ever let me see you again. I will kill you on the spot, and anybody that's with you. Your sister, Bender and Norris will be the only ones to know you're still alive. Now get! Oh, Dean, you come back I'll also kill your sister! I's dead assed serious! Last warning!"

Three hours later and thirty miles north of Tascosa, Dean was having a hard time with Buffalo. "Damnit Buffalo, I need to get home to my wife and kids for a couple of days. Then we'll ride the long way round back for Tascosa. I ain't runnin'! 'Sides that, Gator'll be on the look out for you too."

Buffalo blew his nose, as he turned in the saddle looking at their back trail. "Dean, I know you've got one hell of an orchard to pick with that ass hole. And... don't nobody know this but me and Shorty. That son of a bitch killed my wife two year ago. He's the reason I'm here. Before I leave this country I'm killing him and Booger. Anybody get in my way, or tries to stop me, I'm labile to hurt them too."

Dean looked over and could see the pain on Buffalo's face. "Damn, Buffalo, I'm sorry to hear that. You're right when you say I got some pick'n to do with him. I don't care how he gets it, or who does it as long as he does get buried. I just hope I'm along when he bites the dust. I'll be sure and spit on his body." Dean laughed out loud.

"Hell I'll probably piss on his body if I can hold it long enough while I'm waiting in one hell of a long line. Not only did he steal my cattle, he kidnapped my sister and is holding her against her will. The only reason I've lived this long, is she told him if anything else happens to my family, my property, or me, she'd cut out his nuts when he was asleep. I think he believes her and he is a believer. This is the second time he's cut me loose."

CHAPTER EIGHT

Shorty was sitting on the edge of the bed, pulling on his boots. A loud bang on the door, made him grab for his .45. "Yeah, I'm up! What do you want?"

"This is Mister Farren! Open this door immediately!"

That pissed Shorty off quicker than a skipped heartbeat. "And if I don't want to? I suppose you're going to bust it down, and get shot right in the gut?"

Farren stood there a moment, thinking he'd better change his tone. "I'm sorry, Marshal, but we have ourselves a major problem. I, or that is, we, need your help."

Shorty pulled his other boot on before saying, "I'll be right there." Reaching for his gun belt, he slid it around his waist. With his hat already on his head, he opened the door.

"All right, what kind of a problem do you have?"

"It's Judge Wingate. He didn't arrive at my house last night as scheduled. He's never been late before."

"Uh huh, and why does Judge Wingate stay at your house instead of here in the hotel? Seems kind'a odd to me."

"Well, if you have to know, he's a dear, dear friend of my family. We have known each other for years."

"Uh, huh, I see. Well, this looks like it's going to be a long story, so lets finish it in the café. I ain't had my coffee yet, or breakfast. You hungry?"

"What? Oh, yes, breakfast. I haven't eaten either."

Coffee was poured and their orders were taken before Farren started talking again. "Marshal, I just want you to know, if anything has happened to Judge Wingate, heads will roll. It will start with Johnson, Snyder and their men."

"And why would you think either of those men would have anything to do with something like that?"

"Well, one or the both of them are always bringing false charges of rustling or murder against innocent men. When Judge Wingate does not find them guilty, Johnson and Snyder threaten the law. They have said as much as killing a Judge and town sheriff, would change the situation. It seems as though they must have their way every time. This can not happen!"

"So, what do you want me to do about it?"

"I want you to send men to look for the Judge. You have two innocent men locked in that jail over there. They must be released so they can continue their jobs as Texas Rangers.

"Never, never in all my years of being a man of the courts, have I seen Texas Rangers arrested and charged with murder, just for doing their jobs! It is totally outrageous!"

"Yeah, you keep telling me that. Oh, here comes Johnson and Snyder, now. I'll ask them if they blowed any holes in the judge. My bet is, they didn't and hadn't even thought about it."

Dave and Jack sat at the next table, saying good morning, as they called out for coffee. Jack looked hard at Shorty. "Switching sides, Marshal? Or, do you always eat breakfast with low life, money grubbin' carpetbaggers? "

Farren pushed back his chair and sputtered. "You can't talk about me that way! I won't have it!"

Shorty caught him by his coat sleeve. "Sit the hell down and shut up for a couple of minutes. Maybe you'll learn something."

Shorty drink the last of his coffee, then asked, "Have either of you fellers seen or heard from Judge Wingate? It appears he didn't show up last night as expected."

Dave and Jack looked at each other. Dave smiled, "Naw, but damn, wouldn't it be grand if that bastard got throwed from his buggy and went and got his self killed! Damn, we'd probably have to appoint a new judge that might just be honest. Now that would put the hurt on ole Gator and that damn chinaman."

"Mister Farren wants me to send men out looking for him. Being as it is a judge that's missing, I'd better do it. Say, y'all ain't seen Buffalo and Dean, have you? That might have gotten their asses in a bind. Should'a been here way before now."

"Naw, ain't seen 'em. After breakfast I'll send three or four men looking. Delbert Mangus knows where Dean's place is. They can head that way first. Hope the hell they didn't get caught by Gator and that bunch."

A slight smile crossed Farren's lips. Just last night he had told Rebecca Gordon about Gator and his men already taking care of Buffalo and Dean. That's two less interfering bastards.

"Marshal, I care nothing of your men being unable to find their way back to Tascosa! I want Judge Wingate found!"

Shorty's eyes narrowed. Listen here ass hole! Those two men mean a hell of a lot more to me than nine crooked judges! We'll look for both at the same time. Jack and Dave have enough men in town to do it. Now wait just a damn a minute! Why, all of a sudden did you come to me for help, when you have a town sheriff and Norman, a Texas Ranger?"

"Uh, well it's, uh, they have to stay in town

just to make sure the ranchers don't take the law into their own hands and hang two innocent men."

Jack reached across Dave and Shorty, trying to grab Farren. "You little pip squeak of a human being! I'll yank your damn head off! If I wanted to, I could have already killed both of them! Now shut your mouth in front of me about how innocent them two are. They murdered my brother-in-law, and tow good men before raping my sister! Don't ever, and I mean ever, open your mouth about how innocent they are, in front of me again!"

Farren stood up. "You see, Marshal! They are always threatening an officer of the courts! What is law and order coming to in this world! New laws must be put in place to protect us! Men such as Snyder and Johnson should not be aloud to ride this country as free men! They are a danger to all law officials."

Shorty stood, handing the waitress six bits. "Farren, it ain't the law they hate, it's the crooked men who are trying to enforce their kind of law. You and men like you, and Judge Wingate!"

"I'm leaving! I want a report as soon as any word comes about Judge Wingate. He must be found." Farren hooked 'em.

"Shorty, I'll get men on the trail looking for Dean and Buffalo. Dean may have decided to go home for a few days."

Men were sent to relieve the ones guarding the jail.

Two hours after sun up, men were saddled and ready for the trail. From the south rode a man on a big sorrel horse. Everyone watched as he came down the street. A rifle was in the saddle scabbard, and two pearl handled .45's were on his hips. Whispers floated quietly and quickly among the men. Some let their hands settle on the butt of their own guns, as if already threatened. Everyone knows a gunfighter when they see one. This stranger has got to be a hired killer. Did Gator hire him?

The rider tipped his hat to a couple of smiling women as they started to enter the grocery store. They had stopped, standing still as if taken back by this handsome young man. Never before had either seen a man and his horse with all black gear. His saddle, martingale and bridle, hat, shirt, pants and gun belt, everything, black. What was such a handsome young man doing in Tascosa? Would he stay? Who did he come to see?

To no one's surprise, the rider pulled up in front of the saloon, and dismounted. One of Jacks men had him covered with a doubled barrel shotgun. "Looking for somebody, stranger?"

"Yes, yes I am. Thank you for asking. I'm looking for the town idiot, and I think I've just found him. Yes, I believe I have."

"Well he ain't here! Wait just a damn minute! What do you mean town idiot and you've found him? I don't know nothing about... well shit, let me call Shorty Thompson. He's a U.S Marshal, and he's over there in front of the hotel."

The young man turned his head to look down the street. "Would it be all right if I left my horse tied here? The hitch rail looks pretty well full, in front of the hotel. Now you just run over and fetch the Marshal, while I go in here and have myself a drink. I get mighty thirsty out on the trail."

"Yeah, shor' that's all right. I'll be right back!"

The young man straightened his hat and lifted his pistols just a bit higher in their holsters, after removing the hammer tie down thongs. Riding the horse had settled his guns down. They needed to sit free and loose.

Every man up and down the street had his eyes on this man dressed in black. Men moved, giving room, as he walked toward the bar. He squared himself, removing the glove from his right hand. The young stranger ordered a double shot of rye, and asked for it to be brought to a corner table.

Two minutes later, Shorty walked through the batwing doors. Looking the saloon over, he spotted the stranger at the back table with his drink in his hand. Ordering himself a beer,

Shorty walked over to the table.

The stranger looked up, pushing his hat back, as he set his drink aside. "Are you U.S. Marshal Shorty Thompson?"

Shorty stuck out his hand for a shake. "Yeah, I'm Shorty." They eyed each other a few moments, nether saying a word.

The stranger accepted Shorty's handshake, saying, "Douglas J. Walker. Did you need something, Marshal?"

"Well, no. We was just getting ready to search for Judge Wingate. He's missing. Then the jail guard that was in here eating came and got me. Said there was a stranger in town."

"Yep, that's the truth. I am a stranger. Well I'll say, would you just look at that! Your .45 looks just like this pair of mine! Now if that isn't something. How do you like yours?"

Shorty was taken back with the bold, easy way of this stranger. "Yeah, I like it. Wouldn't have anything else."

"Oh Marshal, before I interrupted you, you were saying something about a missing judge?"

"Yeah, the Circuit Judge was suppose to have been in town last night, and hadn't showed up."

"And I believe you said his name was, Judge Wingate?"

"Yes, that's right. Do you know him?"

Douglas J. Walker looked Shorty in the

eyes. "No, I can't say that I ever met this Judge Wingate. It's a shame too. I think I would have preferred to analyze him for a while. Do you believe him dead, or that he might have heard I was coming and just left the country?" While watching Shorty, Douglas took another drink, and smiled.

Shorty stood there a moment before saying, "I don't know what you're game if feller, but I'll find out when I get back."

Douglas stood up. "This is no game, Mister. I'm dead assed serious. Do you know where to start looking for Wingate, or where you're going? Mighty far between places in these parts."

Shorty had already turned for the door. "Naw, I'd guess anywhere between here and Hayes City."

Douglas pulled his hat forward on his head. "Care if I ride along? I might be able help. Besides that, we can talk."

Shorty looked at him for what seemed minute. "Naw, don't believe so. My back would feel a whole lot better if you wadn't along. But thanks for offering. We'll talk more when I get back."

"Suite yourself. I'll be around for quite a spell." Douglas finished his drink and headed for the hotel.

Just as Shorty and several men got mounted and ready to ride, in rolled the stagecoach. It was a good three hours late.

The driver hollered at Shorty. "Hey feller, with that badge on your shirt, I'd say you're the U.S. Marshal that I'm suppose to talk with when I got here."

Shorty pulled his dun along beside the coach. "Yeah. I'm U.S. Marshal Shorty Thompson. What'da yeh got?"

"I's suppose to tell you that a Judge Wingate went and got his self filled full of lead."

"The hell you say! Where and when did that happen?"

"Over to Hayes City, about three weeks ago. He tried to cut a murdering rustler loose, so the ranchers killed the Judge and the rustler, along with the town marshal. Said they all had to be in on the cattle rustling and the killing of witnesses."

"Well I'll be a suck egg dog! I'll bet ten dollars to one that we have a lawyer here in Tascosa that will have a major barn kicking fit when he hears this bit of news. Yeah, yeah, right along with a town sheriff and a Texas Ranger. And... we got two murdering Deputy Texas Rangers that will have to stay awhile longer in jail. At least until they send another judge. This sure saves us looking for Judge Wingate."

Shorty and Jack Johnson stopped in the café of the hotel for a second cup of coffee. "Just you wait until David Snyder hears about this. He'll damn sure bust a gut laughing. He's hated Judge Wingate since the first trial. Dave had caught two fellers burning hide on a few head of his beefs, and instead of hanging 'em, he brought 'em in. Judge Wingate turned 'em loose, then warned David not to take the law into his own hands again. Men are still considered innocent until a judge and jury find them innocent. None around here have ever been found guilty. David came close to killing him then. I thought they'd lock him up for sure." Jack sure was happy, hearing of the judge's demise.

The stage driver turned the coach and horses over to the hostler at the livery, before heading for the saloon. "Yep, you heard that right! I was there when Judge Wingate was damn near blowed plum' in half. Yep, as I said, I seen it all! Must have been hit by better'n a dozen or more bullets. Hell, he didn't have time to kick mor'n three, maybe four times. Yes sireee, one beautiful sight! Sure hope I live to see something like that again."

Men were crowded all around Don Prather. Of all the years driving a stagecoach, this was the most attention, and drinks he had ever gotten. He was retelling the story to any and all new comers, willing to buy him another drink.

Lawyer Farren came busting through the bat-winged doors. Pushing and shoving men from his path, he reached Prather's side.

Prather was still running his mouth as Farren grabbed him by his shirtfront.

"Prather, Prather! Can you shut the hell up for one stinking minute and let me ask you a few things?"

Prather downed his last shot of whiskey, smiling to himself at how important he had become. "Sure, sure, Lawyer Farren. What is it you need to know?"

"Are you dead sure, positive, that it was Judge Wingate you saw being gunned down!" Farren was pale, with a bead of sweat or two along his upper lip.

"Yep! As I've said before many times. Seen it with my own eyes. Knowed it was him 'cause he rode my coach every other month. And, he was always a nasty bastard sitting back there drunk on his ass, mouth'n off 'cause he was a judge. Been any other passenger and I'd have throwed him off the stage!"

Farren reached, grabbing someone's drink, and slammed it down his throat. Things were not looking to well at the moment. As he left the saloon, he ran into Keefer's deputy.

"Jimmy, I want you to bring Keefer and Ranger Norman to my office at once, now! Hurry, Jimmy, hurry!"

Keefer was still in bed, and told Jimmy he had to go eat breakfast first. Norman was dead assed drunk and it took two buckets of water to bring him around. "Mister Farren said for y'all to hurry. He seemed all in a tether."

"You just tell him to keep his damned shirt on! We'll be there after breakfast!" Norman had one hell of a headache.

Jimmy delivered Norman's message to a screaming idiot. "You go back and tell both of them stupid bastards... forget it! I'll go to the café and talk with them there!"

Farren was on his second cup of coffee when both Keefer and Norman came in ordering black coffee. "Judge Wingate is dead! It'll take several weeks to get him replaced with someone we have control of. If for any reason another judge is sent here in the mean time, Jeb and Ned will talk their damned heads off, before they hang. Along with that, both of you will be found out, and then we all will hang. After breakfast, I want you both to ride to Jun Dung and Gator. Tell them about Judge Wingate, and ask what we should do about Jeb and Ned. Get back to me as soon as you can. We all may have to leave here in a hurry."

Farren got up to leave, but changed his mind and sit back down. "I almost forgot. Be sure and tell them it's been over three weeks since Judge Wingate's death. Another judge may well be on his way here now. It might be best if they had men camped on all trails and roads leading to Tascosa and get rid of anyone that even looks like a judge. Time could be short, so hurry."

An hour before sundown, Keefer and Norman were back from seeing Gator, and was in Farren's office. Norman was wiping sweat from his face, as Keefer talked. "Damnit I don't know what Gator and that bunch is going to do! Gator said he'd handle it and for us to get our asses back here. He said it would be taken care of tonight, ever what that means."

Farren was walking the floor again. "Maybe one of y'all should go over and talk with Jeb and Ned. Just reassure them we'll get them out somehow. Let them know Gator is handling everything. I don't think either of them trust me. Norman, it might be best if it was you. After all, they are your men."

Norman stopped wiping his face, saying, "my men my ass! Gator sent them here to do a job! I didn't hire them! But I'll do it. Yeah, I'll do it. It might look better if I went to see my deputies."

Norman opened the front door to leave Farren's office, when down the street rode fifty or sixty men. With horses in a dead run, they fired at anything, and everyone they saw. As Shorty and Jack stepped from the saloon, Jack and David's men were returning fire. Dropping behind the horse trough, Shorty and every one of the other men opened fire.

After only two quick passes up and down the street firing every gun they had, and loosing over fifteen men, the raiders left town in a cloud of dust.

Shorty had glanced toward the hotel and saw the young gunman, Douglas J Walker, standing on the walkway with his .45's in both hands. He had killed several of the riders, and had a smile on his face. Walker flipped open the cylinders of his pistols, and inserted new bullets.

Shorty made his way among dead men and dying horses, to stand beside Walker. "Kind'a fancy shooting, feller."

Walker smiled. "You weren't doing so bad yourself. Uh huh. Even if you were lying on your belly, hid behind a water trough. Yeah, damn good shooting, from that position."

Shorty bowed up. "What in the hell do you think I should have done? Stood up and got my ass shot off! Only an idiot would even think of doing a thing like that!"

The smile left Walker's face. "You wouldn't happen to be calling me an idiot, would you?"

"Naw, I wouldn't say that." Shorty looked him in the eye. Hell yes I'll say that! You was a damned idiot, looking for death!"

Their eyes locked for several seconds. Walker smiled first. "Yeah, you're right. But damned, that is the most fun I've had in several years. Killing murdering bastards sure is exhilarating."

"I still haven't got around to finding out what you're up to. I kind'a figgered you was on the other side of the law."

"And why would you think that? Is it the way I dress? Oh, never mind." Pointing across the street at Farren's office, Walker asked, "Do you know anything about that lawyer, Farren?"

"Naw, not much. Just that all his clients are outlaws, and his best buddies are a Texas Ranger that goes by the handle of 'Norman', and the local sheriff called Keefer. Maybe I'm wrong, but I'd say they both are as crooked as a dog's hind leg."

"Well I'll say, friends of Ranger Raymond Wendal Norman. Now if that don't beat all. Would you happen to know them well enough to introduce us? I'd like to meet this Ranger Norman."

Shorty looked at him, saying, "yeah, I'll introduce y'all, but so you'll know, they damned sure ain't my friends!"

"That's fine. Mighty fine. When would you like to do this?"

"Hell, right now. We'll just walk into his office."

Keefer and Norman were sitting, as Farren walked the floor. "Just why in the hell would Gator ride in here and think he could just take Jeb and Ned out of that jail? Unless, unless you idiots didn't tell him about a U.S Marshal, and all of Johnson's and Snyder's men being in town!"

Keefer looked at Norman, then said, "you never said a word about us telling him that!

You told us to tell him Wingate was dead and that he should put men on the roads and trails! That's all you said to tell him! That's it, so don't blame us!"

"You idiots, I'm not blaming you, but Gator sure as hell will! And if I know hi…" Before Farren finished the sentence, a loud knock on the door, brought total quiet to the room. Farren looked around before saying, "the door's open. Come on in."

Shorty and Walker walked in.

Farren turned red with rage. "And what in the hell are you doing here, and what do you want, Marshal?"

"This man wanted an introduction to you ass holes." Pointing to each one, Shorty started out with Walker. "This is Douglas J. Walker, and that is Lawyer Farren, Sheriff Keefer, and Texas Ranger Raymond Wendal Norman."

Walker stuck out his hand to Farren, then to Keefer, saying it was a pleasure to meet them. When he got to the extended hand of Norman's, he drew one of his .45's so fast no one saw it until it came crashing down on Norman's skull, knocking him cold as a week old fart. He dropped like a turd in an outhouse.

Shorty's mouth was open, as Farren screamed, "What in the hell did you do that for? Are you a crazy man?"

Putting away his pistol, Walker smiled. "Yeah, I'd say more than one person probably thinks that. Marshal Shorty, what would you say to helping me drag this bastard across the street to jail? Or should we wait until he comes to, and make him walk?"

Without knowing, Shorty had pulled his .45. "What I'd like to know is why in the hell you did that?"

"Oh, forgive me. Did I forget to mention, Texas Ranger Raymond Wendal Norman was my uncle? I found him shot in the back of the head. He was still in his bedroll, and couldn't have seen it coming. With all of his papers gone, I figured someone would try using his identity to pose as a ranger. That's him."

Keefer and Farren looked at each other, then both tried talking at once. Farren won out. "Well the dirty, murdering, no good scoundrel! Thank God you found him before he could do any more harm. We, that is, neither Sheriff Keefer nor myself knew anything about his background. We believed him to be a ranger. Once he's in jail, I'll come over later and question him."

After a bucket of water was poured in his face, Norman, or rather Reyes, came to. "Why in the hell did you do that, Mister?"

"Because you are a back shooting, murdering bastard! That's why. You killed the real Ranger Norman."

"Naw, naw, it wadn't me! It was..." Knowing he was dead if he opened his mouth, he shut up, asking, "what are you gonna do with me? You have no proof who done it! Wadn't me!"

"You are going to jail, and wait trial. Let's go!"

When Shorty and Walker hit the walkway with their prisoner, Farren was already talking to Keefer. "Get your ass to Gator and tell him what has happened! The whole shitting world is coming down around our ears!"

A knock on the back door stunned Farren for just a moment. "Who, who is it?"

"Gator and Booger, you dumb shit! Open this damn door before I kick it down!"

As the door was opened, Farren started explaining, "Now Gator, it ain't what you thin..."

Gator stopped him in mid-sentence. "What in the hell are you trying to do, wipe out my whole outfit? Why in the hell wasn't I told there was over a hundred men in town? And, who in the hell was that ass hole standing in front of the hotel with both guns blazing? Damnit I lost damn near twenty men! We've still got to get Jeb and Ned out of that jail."

"Gator, Gator, you've got to listen to me! Now!"

"All right, what the hell is it?"

"We got a bigger problem than just Jeb and Ned."

Booger bounced right in front of Farren. "Just what in the hell could be worse than two ass holes about to spill their gut to the law? Just tell us, what?"

Farren was weakening fast. His legs could no longer hold him up, and his voice was shaking. "It's Norman, I mean Reyes. The real Ranger Norman's nephew came in here and knocked Reyes cold, and him and a U.S. Marshal dragged him over and locked him up with Jeb and Ned. It looks bad, Gator, bad."

Gator and Booger looked at each other for a full minute before Gator said, "why in the hell wasn't we told when a U.S. Marshal showed up here? Damnit all to hell! When another judge gets here... You are going to be able to get a judge to take Wingate's place, ain't you?"

Farren paled just a bit more. "Yes, oh yes, of course. Now you have to realize it'll take a little more time. We have a Judge Thomas that has worked with the family for years. I can get him, but it might take close to a month to get him here."

Gator wiped his face with his hand, thinking. "Okay, you get on that today! I mean get the letter on the next stage out of here! Now, in the mean time, like right now, I want you to get Rebecca over here. I need her to do a little job for me."

"But, but I don't know where she'd be this time of evening. She rides a lot to get away from that doctor. She may be in bed."

"You idiot! You get on the letter to Judge Thomas, and this stupid piece of shit you call the sheriff, can find Rebecca, and get her over here, now! Be best if me and Booger stay out of sight. Move! Damnit, we ain't got forever! And bring us something to eat. We ain't eat a damn bite today. And bring us a bottle!"

Keefer almost fell on his face in his hurry to get out of there. Mumbling and grumbling to himself, he headed for Doctor Gordon's house. "Call me a piece of shit, will he! They'd better watch who they're talking to, I run this town! I'm the sheriff! I give orders I don't take 'em from nobody! They don't want to piss me off. There is a whole lot I can do. They think them other boys can talk! Wait until the nut crunchin' starts, they'll be in my jail!"

Doctor Gordon, sleepy eyed, opened the front door. "Keefer? What in the world do you want, this time of night?"

"Sorry as I can be, Doc, but we need Mrs. Gordon to come over to Mister Farren's office and tell what she saw this afternoon. Shouldn't take all that long."

Doc got angry. "I think you and Mister Farren are a couple of bumbling idiots! Rebecca is in bed, asleep! Come morning, I'll ask her if she has anything to say to you. Good night, Sir!"

Keefer mumbled to himself all the way back to Farren's office. "I'll show 'em! You wait and see. I should have grabbed that snotty Doctor and shoved him out of the way, and went in and got Rebecca myself. Before this is over, she'll be mine! I know she likes me. I caught her looking at me one time, and if they'll look once, they'll do it again."

"Where in the hell is Rebecca?" Gator was pissed off.

"The Doc came to the door, and said she was already in bed and asleep. Said he'd tell her in the morning."

"All right, we'd better get some sleep ourselves. Tomorrow might be one hell of a long day. Oh, we're camping at your place, Farren. Like I said, we gotta stay out of sight."

Farren cringed at the thought of these filthy, grimy men staying in his nice, clean home. "My God! I forgot..." He again, paled and got weak in the knees.

Booger grabbed him and spun him all the way around. "Forgot what? Damnit, forgot what?"

"No, no, it has nothing to do with any of this. It's just that Doctor Gordon's daughter is at my house with my dinner ready. I am afraid she will be angry, for me being late."

Gator smiled right big, frightening Farren just a bit more. "Well I'll say, so you've been snorting the flanks of the Doc's daughter, while your sweet-heart is married to the Doc. I wonder if she gets more out of it than you do?" He laughed like a fool. "I think before this is over, I'll get a little bit from of them both."

Farren found at least one slim bit of bravery. "Gator, if you of Booger lay a hand on ei-

ther one of those women, I'll kill you myself."
For some reason, there was no quiver in his
voice, as he looked both of them in the eye.
"Those are two frail, delicate ladies, and should
never be confronted by the likes of you!"

Instead of being mad, Gator laughed.
"Well hardy, har, har! When they spread their
legs, I'll see just how delicate they are!"

Farren was just now finding out what kind
of men he had tied himself, and Rebecca up
with. Why would Rebecca bring him here to
this lawless country? "That's right, it was
Rebecca all along that insisted on coming to
Tascosa. I must talk with Jun Dung, and see if
he can control these, these, whatever they are.
If not, I'll quietly get Rebecca, and get the hell
out of Tascosa."

Half the money from the stolen cattle would
be nice, but being killed by murdering outlaws... And Rebecca could even be raped and
savaged by these filthy, evil men. Tomorrow,
yes tomorrow he would have his talk with Jun
Dung, and Rebecca. Rebecca must be ready
to leave at a moment's notice.

"Hey Farren, wake up! You day dream'n
'er something? Mumbling yer ass off. I said
me and Booger are head'n for your place. You
drop by the saloon and fetch us a couple of
bottles. We'll see if the Doc's daughter is still
there with supper on the table so we can eat. I
just hope she's good lookin'."

"What'll it be, Mister Farren?" The bartender had a towel in his left hand, and an empty glass in his right.

"Oh, hello, Ed. I'll have a bottle of Rye, make it two, unopened, and yes, I'll have a double shot now."

"You don't look real good, Mister Farren. Maybe you should drop by and see Doc Gordon, tomorrow."

"Thank you Ed, I'll do just that." Farren headed for the bat-winged door, as Shorty and Walker came through. Just for a moment, Farren had a glimmer of hope, but dismissed it, glancing back at Shorty twice before the doors closed behind him.

Shorty had seen something in Farren's eyes that had not been there before. Until now, he has had a look of arrogance, even power, along with a snotty attitude. But that look was a look of desperation and fear. Shorty had seen it before, in many men.

Sitting with David Snyder, and Jack Johnson. Shorty and Walker ordered a drink. "Well Shorty, when do think we can get us another judge in here? Now I don't mean one that's on Gator's payroll. I mean a honest to goodness judge." Johnson knew he and David had to get their men back to their ranches. They couldn't stay in Tascosa to many days.

"Jack, I don't know. But you know as well as I do, Wingate getting killed was the best thing that could have happened. I'll get a wire on the stage to President Hayes. It'll have to go by coach to Hayes City, then the telegraph operator can send it."

Walker was taking everything in. Just sipping his drink, he never missed a sentence or statement from anyone. "Gentlemen, about how many honest men and women would you say live in these parts? By honest, I mean not on someone's payroll."

"What in the hell does that have to do with anything?" David wanted to go over to the jail and take every one of those ass holes out and hang them, now.

Walker looked to each man sitting around the table. "Well, in a pinch, it could mean lives. If you know the ones not to trust, and the ones you can, you're one hell of a lot farther ahead."

Jack finished his beer, before saying, "we know most of the damned spies around here, but I believe there are a few more. Me and David both might have one or two working for us."

"Well gentlemen, knowing who you can thust is important. I'm going to sleep on it. Goodnight." Walker finished his drink and headed upstairs to his room.

Farren walked into his living room, and handed a bottle of rye to Gator. "Where's Miss Gordon? Have both of you eaten?"

Gator smiled that wicked smile of his. "Yeah, we've eat. The Gordon woman is in the kitchen, keeping your supper warm."

Farren entered the kitchen, and walked over to kiss Mildred on the cheek. "I'm sorry I'm late, dear. I just had a lot to do tonight. Several clients were late getting into town. How are you doing this evening? You look well."

"Yes, yes, I'm fine. Eat your supper before it gets cold, and we'll talk while you eat. "Those gentlemen said they were out of town clients of yours and were going to stay a few days with you. After finishing their meal, they excused themselves and said they would wait for you in the sitting room and smoke. I guess this means I won't be able to spend the next few nights with you. Maybe you can drop by my house for a short bit, tomorrow night. I must go dear, but goodness me, I haven't let you say a word."

Farren pushed back his plate. You are such a dear. It won't be long until we are together, always. I'll walk you home."

"Thank you dear, but you must stay with your guest."

Farren walked into the sitting room. "Gator, I want to thank you and Booger for being nice to Mildred, uh, Miss Gordon."

Gator looked at him. "Yeah, it'd have stirred up shit."

"You could be in more shit than you think. That man that was riding with Dean, that you killed, was a Deputy U.S. Marshal."

Gator bolted to the floor. "How in the hell do you know this? We didn't kill him and Dean, but I guess we should'a. I should'a took care of Dean months ago! Booger, come morning, I want you to take three or four men and ride to Dean's place and kill the whole damn family! Yeah, and the damn Marshal, too."

Mildred Gordon had been gone no more than five minutes, when there was a knock on the back door. Gator and Booger both pulled their guns. "Put those damn guns away! That is most likely a neighbor. I'll go talk to him." Farren hissed.

Farren opened the door, and in walked Nate. "Sorry I was so long getting here, but there was too many people about. I didn't want to be seen. You did know that Jack, David and their whole damn bunch of hands are in town."

"Yeah, we know. Gator and Booger are in the sitting room. We're trying to figure out what to do about Jeb, Ned and Reyes. All three of them are in jail."

Gator heard them talking and hollered. "Y'all come on in here. Nate, did you know all them ranchers was going to be in town today? Damn near got us all killed."

"No, heck no! I last seen them riding for Johnson's place. What are you going to do about the boys that are in jail?"

That stupid smile of Gator's crossed his

face. "Not to worry yer head off. I'll have that took care of tomorrow. Just as soon as I see Rebecca, I'll get her to find out where our boys are sitting, and we'll bust 'em out. One hell of a lot of commotion in the street, and with a strong horse or two and rope, we'll yank them damn bars plum' off the back of that jail."

Nate took a drink from the bottle, then said, "She ought'a know where they're sitting now. I could go over to Gordon's and ask her. Probably piss of Doc, though."

"Yeah, but she's asleep. We've already been there."

Nate looked surprised. "Naw, she ain't asleep. I just saw her ten minutes ago, coming out the back door of the jail."

Every man in the room stood up. Keefer went wild eyed. "Naw, naw, that can't be true, Gator! Now damnit, I truly went and talked with Doc. He told me…"

"Shut the hell up for a minute! Let me think. What in the hell would she be doing coming out the back door of the jail?" Gator scratched his beard a couple of times, as Farren walked the floor.

"Well' there ain't nothing more we can do tonight, lets hit the sack and see how tomorrow starts out. Could be a mighty interesting day. I'll talk with Rebecca tomorrow."

CHAPTER NINE

Men were lined up in front of both cafés, waiting their turn for breakfast. Glen, one of the men guarding the jail, had finished his breakfast, but stopped to talk with his boss. "Jack, you know it's a funny thing, them three fellers hollered and made noise half the damn night. Now I can't even get 'em awake to go to the outhouse. Guess when they get hungry, they'll let somebody know. Well, I'd better get back so Oscar can come and eat. The cook told us to come around to the back door and just walk on in."

Jack hollered at him before he got out the door. "Glen, don't just one of you boys take them to the outhouse. Holler out and get more help. And keep your guns in your hands, ready for use. Somebody might try and snatch them from you. Oh, and I want two men guarding them at all times. Only one of you come and get their breakfast and coffee, when they're ready."

A second cup of coffee was being poured, when in walked Walker. Glancing around the room, he spotted Shorty, Jack and David. As a man got up from the next table, Walker grabbed his chair and set it between Jack and Shorty.

"Morning, gentlemen. How's the coffee. Looks like a tight place to eat this morning. Jack, when are you and David going to send some of your men back to your ranches?"

David looked at him, over his cup of coffee. "Not that it's any of your damn business, but when we get damned good and ready. Walker, you seem like a reasonable feller, why did you come to Tascosa and put your nose in the middle of everything?"

Walker lowered his coffee cup, and smiled. "Then all of you think I'm a bit too nosey for my own good? Is that it?"

David looked about the table at the other men, and when no one answered Walker, he did. "Yeah, I'd go that far in saying that. Here you are a total stranger, and just stepped into our group like you was part of it. We can't take a piss without you being there to watch. We drink a beer you drink Rye. We drink coffee, have breakfast, you show up. Now you might just be lonesome, but I don't think so. I think you're up to something, and just pumping us for the information you need. That about right?"

Shorty was sitting with a little smile on his face. Walker asked, "Is that the way you and Jack feel, Shorty? If you don't want me about, all you have to do is tell me. I'm sure I can find other friends. After all, I'll be in Tascosa for a good while."

Shorty waved off the waiter from bringing more coffee. "Walker, I still haven't figgered you out yet. You ride in here and help with a gunfight, split the skull of a fake Texas Ranger, and then you tell me the real Ranger was your uncle. You also said you came upon your uncle's body while he was still in his bedroll. How was it you were trailing your uncle?"

Walker looked to each man. "Then what you're saying, is you don't trust me, and it would be better if I left Tascosa."

"Naw, now we ain't saying that. It's just, well, what are you going to do for a living, around here? Just, well, what in the hell are you here for? You sure as hell don't look like a cowboy, nor a banker. Could you be a gunfighter?"

"Could you fellows wait a few minutes, while I go up to my room. I think it's time I showed you something. Better yet, will the three of you come up to my room?"

Shorty looked at Jack and David. "Yeah, I guess we can, but it'd better be good."

They got to the room, and David stood with his hands on his hips. "So, you've got yourself a black coat to match your riding gear. What in the hell does that have to do with anything?"

Walker laughed out loud. "No, it's not a coat, it's a robe, to go with this." He opened his valise and uncovered a large, heavy wooden plaque that read, DOUGLAS J. WALKER, U.S. CIRCUIT JUDGE, DISTRICT 9, at large. "Gentlemen, I am the new Circuit Judge you have been waiting for. And Shorty, President Hayes also appointed me. David, before you ask, at large means that I do not hold court in any one courthouse. I travel the western states of the United States. I hold court wherever appropriate. I'm very sorry I had to mislead you for a while, but President Hayes' advisors told me it would be best if I kept my identity to myself, until I found who could and could not be trusted."

"How in the hell did you know it was President Hayes that appointed me? And knowing that, why didn't you come to me?"

"If I hadn't found uncle Raymond dead, I most likely would have looked you up at once, as the President told me you would be on this case. But at first, I didn't know if you were the real U.S. Marshal M D Thompson or not. The same men that killed uncle Raymond, could have killed you and planted someone in your place. I had no way of knowing."

Jack finely found his voice. "Answer me something, why in the hell did you come riding in here all dressed in black, with two forty-fives on your hips? Why would a Circuit Judge risk his life in a gun fight with a bunch of raiders?"

"Oh, that. Well I've always wanted to be a

gunfighter, and if not for my uncle Raymond, I might have been. By dressing this way, and keeping my identity secret for a week or so, I can enter a town and find out a great deal about the criminal element without anyone knowing what I am. I have found out west, there are as many crooked lawmen as honest ones. In order to live a bit longer, I'll do things my way."

"What are you going to do about them bastards over there in jail?" Jack felt somewhat better about judges, right now.

"If all of you would like, we can go by Lawyer Farren's office and see if he is going to represent the defendants. If he does, I will hold court as soon as he has their defense in order. If Farren is not going to represent them, I must give them the appropriate time to find a lawyer. They should have one. Oh, we also can go by the jail and tell the men that they are officially charged with murder, and rape. Perhaps one of them will turn on the others and tell the court everything. I think Reyes will talk."

"Yes, of course, I'll represent them, just as soon as Judge Henry Thomas arrives. He will be here in less than a month."

Farren slapped his coat pocket, he still had the letter to Judge Thomas, and now realized he had forgotten to mail it, and the stage was gone. Gator must not know. God, no one can know! He needed to talk with Rebecca.

Shorty smiled. "Mister Farren, this young

gentleman is the new U S. Circuit Judge. Douglas J. Walker. Sure saves a lot of time, don't you think?"

Farren paled and reached for a chair. "No, no, that can't be true! I have sent for Judge Henry Thomas! How can this be? We only found that Judge Wingate was murdered! How did this happen so suddenly? Surely you are joking? Too beat that, I personally saw this man stand on the hotel porch and kill several men. No, no, this isn't right!"

Judge Walker looked at everyone, almost shocked at the response from Farren. "Mister Farren, it is true. President Hayes sent me here to replace Judge Wingate, and investigate him and his bench. We didn't know he was dead. I was to go over all court documents in which Judge Wingate has presided. The records show there were too many irregularities in his proceedings. His records, if any, will be sent to Washington."

Farren wanted to pass out cold. "No, no, that can't be! How can anyone think such a thing? Judge Wingate was a dedicated Court Official. I simply can not believe this!"

David wanted to reach over and jerk his damned head plumb off his shoulders. "Just you listen here to me you little pip-squeak, you are the ass hole that defended those outlaw bastards! Maybe somebody should investigate you!"

"Hold on there Mister Snyder! This man

was just doing his job, his duty, by defending any and all accused. Everyone is considered innocent until proven guilty in a court of law. They must be represented by a defense, that is the law."

Jack had to laugh. "Boy howdy, the last crooks through the court in Tascosa, sure was defended. With three or more witnesses against them, they'd still get off bird free, and the fellers that brought 'em in was told not to take the law into their own hands no more. We should'a hung all of 'em, stead of bringing 'em in here to be turned loose by a crooked judge!"

Gunfire in the street brought Walker and Shorty in a run. Jack and David were close on their heels. One of Jack's men was in the street, in front of the jail, firing one shot at a time into the air. Seeing Jack and the other men leaving Lawyer Farren's office, he headed toward them in a run, shouting all the way.

"Jack, Jack, y'all ain't going to believe this, but all three of them fellers in jail are dead! Damnit, that's why I couldn't wake them for breakfast, they was all dead!"

Everyone had stopped in their tracks. Shorty spoke first. "All right, Oscar, you head over and get Doc Gordon. Pete, why don't you go get the undertaker? Damn, this gets deeper and deeper. Jack, Walker, we may's well go on over and check this out. I wonder what happened. Hell, they was healthy."

Entering the jail, Jack's guard started talking as fast as Oscar had. "Now Jack, before anybody starts looking at me and Oscar, we had nothing to with them dying. And, we heard no shots last night. 'Course they don't have any bullet holes either. It's a horrible looking sight, them staring straight up, with their eyes wide open. Ain't seen nothing like it before."

Shorty leaned over and smelled Reyes' mouth. Smells kind'a like cyanide to me. Never smelled it on a man before, but a feller in Wyoming was using it to kill wolves, and I smelled it then. Oh, here's the doc."

Doctor Gordon and Farren came rushing through the doorway. Farren's mouth was already working overtime. "This time you've gone too far! Johnson, you and Snyder can expect a call from a U.S. Marshal! I'll have them here befo... Oh, we have one, don't we?" Farren, in his frightened haste to get Jack and David, had forgotten about Shorty and Judge Walker.

Clearing his mind, he shouted, "Marshal, I demand you arrest these two men, now! Murder will not go unpunished!"

David stepped in front of him. "Well it has until now, you stupid little shit! You shor' as hell ain't going to get these three off. Looks to me as if somebody saved us a hanging."

Doctor Gordon rose from his knees, saying, "Someone gave them enough poison to kill a dozen horses. Wasn't no accident. They was meant to die. I'd say it was plenty painful, ought'a been hollering their heads off for a good hour before death. Somebody knowed what they was doing."

"Doc, how could you get grown men to take cyanide?" Shorty was sitting on his heels, looking the cell over.

"Hard to say. I'd guess in their food, or even dissolved in their water. Now it'd likely smell in water, but not food."

The undertaker had walked in and heard Doc's words. "Doctor Gordon, want I should cut 'em open and see what they eat? No longer than they been dead, wouldn't take much to tell. It'd be no extra charge to the town."

Doc Gordon looked at Shorty. What do you think, Marshal?"

"I can't see where it'd help. That wouldn't tell us who done it. Oscar, where did y'all get their food, last night?"

"Over at the hotel café, same as always."

Oscar thought a minute, then blurted out, "Now hold on Marshal! Don't you go thinking Mrs. Marsden had anything to do with killing these fellers! I've knowed her since coming west. Ain't no way she'd done this!"

Shorty smiled. "Naw, Oscar, I wadn't thinking nothing like that. I was just wondering if somebody else could have got their hands on the food for a couple of minutes."

141

"Wadn't no way. I stood in the kitchen door-way talking, the whole time she was cooking. And, nobody else was there, then I brung it right on over here. No Sir! No way."

Judge Walker hadn't said a word, he was thinking. "Gentlemen, why don't we look at everything from another perspective. As we know..." He was cut off in mid-sentence.

David had his hands on his hips. Douglas, er, I mean Judge, why in the hell don't you talk English? What in the hell is this 'perspective'? Is that kind'a like another angle?"

"That is exactly what it means. Now, nei-ther Jack, nor David killed them. If they'd wanted to do it, they'd have done it days ago instead of bringing them in to the law. Which by the way if it had been me, I'd hung them on the spot, after filling them with lead. So, what if ever who did it, did it to keep them from talk-ing? All the ranchers knew Judge Wingate was dead, so they would probably have a better chance of getting a conviction with a new judge. So you see, I'd be looking elsewhere for the murderers."

Men were helping the undertaker remove the bodies. Everyone else was in deep thought. Jack removed his hat and scratched his head. "All of this means we have to start at zero, getting Gator and Bugger, along with that damn chinaman. Well, maybe not plum' zero, but pretty damn close."

CHAPTER TEN

Booger pulled his horse to a sliding halt. He had seen riders coming their way. "Well lookey yonder, fellers! I'd be damned if that ain't Dean and that Deputy, headed right for us. Saves us a lot of riding. Two of y'all get your horses out of sight over there in that arroyo. Nate, you come with me."

Starting to ride off, he hollered back, "Now damnit, don't kill 'em! Shoot 'em up a little if you have to, but don't kill 'em."

As Booger and Nate turned west, to ride behind a small rise, Buffalo had seen light reflection on moving metal. "Hold it Dean! I just saw sunlight on steel. Somebody is setting a trap for us. Would you think it'd be Gator and his bunch?"

"Yeah, I sure's hell would! Where bouts did you see that reflection? I know this country pretty damn good. Just maybe we can reverse this trap."

"Off to the west of the trail. Can you see that low rise about six hundred yards out there? It looked to be moving in that direction. Wonder how many there is?"

Dean pulled his rifle from the scabbard, jacking a shell into the chamber. "Never less than four, no, never less than four. Okay, Buffalo, we have a pretty deep gulch we'll be riding down into before we get to that knoll. Now that gulch runs east about a hundred yards from the trail, then turns south toward the river, becoming a deeper arroyo. My guess is that they'd have two men in the arroyo, and two more would be behind that knoll.

"That arroyo has a sandy bottom, so they can't hear us coming. I'd like to ride down easy like, until we see them, then blow holes in them two before getting off our horses to shoot the next bastards that will be coming like a bat out of hell from behind that knoll. What do you think?"

Buffalo had his rifle in his hands. "Sounds good to me, but Dean, if all possible, don't kill Gator. I need that bastard, bad!"

"Shit, Buffalo, we don't know if it's Gator, or who. I'm gonna blow the ass off anybody I see. Look, Look! One of the ass holes just rode into sight on top of the knoll. He must'a thought we couldn't see him. Okay, here's the gulch. They're watching, so ride straight ahead into the gulch out of sight, before turning east. Ain't gonna be long now."

Riding east a short distance, then back south, Buffalo saw two horses tied to a scrub cedar. "Pssst, pssst, Dean. There they are. Let's both fire at once. You take the one on the left. Dean, if you can keep from it, don't kill 'em."

Dean raised his rifle to his shoulder. "Fire on three. One, two, three!" As the men dropped, Dean and Buffalo kicked their horses into a run to cut the short distance between them. Dismounting on the run, Dean grabbed one man, while Buffalo grabbed the other.

Dean had shot his in the right forearm, while Buffalo had bounced a bullet of the back of the other's head. "Damn, Buffalo, I thought you'd blowed his damn head off."

"Naw, I just gave him a headache. He'll be out for a spell. Let's ask yours who is with them and who put them up to ambushing us. Wait! Here they come, now! They probably think these two ass holes got us."

Booger and Nate rode into the arroyo, before realizing that Buffalo and Dean had them covered. Nate raised his hands, but Booger went for his pistol.

Buffalo knocked him from his saddle with the stock of his rifle. Jumping from his horse, he grabbed Booger's pistol, throwing it fifty yards into the weeds.

Booger slowly got to his knees, then stood with a look of hate on his face. "What in the hell did y'all do that for? We was just going to grab y'all and take you to Gator, again."

"Yeah, in a big fat pigs ass you would have! Both these boys here had cocked rifles. They was told to blow holes in us, and you're the one that told them to do it."

"Naw, naw, now Dean, you got me all wrong. I always liked you. Why, I even told your sister that just the other day. Next time you see..." Hummph.

Buffalo had hit Booger in the side of the head so hard he fell to the sand in a heap, not even trying to break his fall. As Dean was watching this happen, Nate went for his gun, and got a bullet in the arm for his trouble.

"Damnit Dean! You didn't have to shoot me! I was just gonn'a disarm y'all and ride off! You know me, Dean!"

"Yeah, I know you, and am finding out more about you every day. You're going to see David. You turn coat, lyin'shit!"

Booger came to and was as mad as a raging bull. "You stupid bastard, what did you do that for? I ain't done one damn thing to you! We even let you go when you was caught with Dean, snooping around. Just what in the hell is your bitch with me?"

"I'll tell you, and then I'm going to beat you to death with my bare hands. Two years ago, you and Gator and your gang of cutthroats came by my ranch and killed my wife! You were dressed as soldiers and we watered your horses, and fed y'all before you turned on us, killing everyone that moved. I was shot and left for dead. Me and my partner tracked y'all to San Francisco, but y'all jumped a ship to China. I'm killing you both!"

"Yeah, I 'member that. When I shot you, you dropped like a wounded buffalo. Shame Gator had to kill your wife, we both wanted to pump on her first. And with that gun in your hand you can probably kill me! But, if you put that gun down and I'll rip your damn head off!" Booger was big and mean.

Buffalo removed his gun belt, and looped it around his saddle horn. Walking straight at Booger, he feinted with a left to the face, while using his right for an upper cut to the crotch. Dropping to his knees, both of Booger's hands went between his legs as Buffalo busted his nose with the toe of his right boot.

Booger was flat on his back, with one hand covering what was left of his balls, the other over his nose. Two hard kicks to the ribs, and one good head snapping shot to the side of the head, Booger was out cold. Buffalo stood over him a good three minutes, wanting him to move one more time.

"Nate, get your damn rope down here and tie this ass hole up. And it'd better be good. If he gets loose, I'll shoot you first."

Buffalo was strapping his gun belt around his waist. Dean was still holding his cocked rifle on Nate, and the other two, while watching Buffalo put the hurt on Booger. "Damn, Buffalo, I always thought Booger was the meanest bastard around Tascosa, but he never got one swing. What'er you going to do with him?"

"I want to kill him so damn bad it hurts. I promised my dead wife, that if I ever found this bastard and Gator, I'd kill them with my bare hands. But damnit, that'd be too quick. I want 'em to suffer a few years before they die, maybe in some prison. We'll take these fellers into Tascosa, and ask Shorty what we should do with them. If that damned Judge Wingate thinks he can turn 'em loose, I'll shoot him. Anyhow, it'll be up to Shorty."

As Nate tied Booger, and the other two men, he blurted out. "I guess y'all hadn't heard, but Wingate was killed over to Hayes City. And Dean, I ain't never done you no wrong. Why can't you just turn your back and let me ride off?"

"Because you are a worthless sack of shit! I'd have to live with myself, and I don't think I could, knowing you was out there somewhere back stabbing some other bunch of friends that trusted you. Naw, I'm taking you to David Snyder."

CHAPTER ELEVEN

"Rebecca, it's over, finished! We've got to get out of here, now!" Farren was pleading; he and Rebecca must leave Tascosa before Doc Gordon got through with the mess at the jail. "That little U.S. Marshal, and that damned judge are just too smart.

"Hurry, I'll help you grab a few things, then we'll drop by my house and office for my money and a few clothes."

Rebecca was sitting on the edge of Doctor Gordon's bed, brushing her hair. "Darling, if you think for one minute I'm going to leave here before those cattle are taken to Hayes City and sold, you've got another think coming! Twenty-five per-cent of that money is mine! Besides that, no one suspects me of anything. I am the loving wife of Doctor Gordon! Now, if I were you, I'd get Gator and Booger to go ahead and kill that Chinaman, and get those cattle sold, now! What is taking them so long?"

Farren was thinking hard, and very shaken.

"But dear, you don't understand. Reyes and his men that were in jail are dead! Someone poisoned them!" Who could have done such a thing?"

Moving from the bed to a chair in front of the huge mirror, Rebecca continued brushing her hair. "Yes darling, that is what everyone is, and will be asking, who could have done such a thing? Well I did! All I had to do was rub up against Oscar, and brush his lips with mine. Men are so stupid! He has no idea it was me that dropped that poison in that food. And he won't say a word about me being there. I promised him a short lay in the hay if no one could possible find out about it."

Rebecca was smiling, and Farren had a deep scowl on his face. She looked up and saw his expression. "Don't look so shocked and hurt. I'd screw the preacher's balls off to get my ranch back, and the money I've got coming. So keep your trap shut and get out to the ranch! Tell them to get those cattle moving as soon as possible! After they're on the trail a couple of days, send Nate back in to tell me. He'd ride through gunfire just to look at my chest. I'll go for my normal ride and keep going."

"You! It was you that poisoned those men! How could you be so cold hearted, killing our own men?" Farren was shocked.

"Yes, screwing them to death would have

taken a bit too long. And I know you darling; you would have let them talk us on to the hanging tree! I shut them up, for good! Now get out of here before someone sees you! Damnit, quit looking like a whipped pup! If you play this right, you'll still have me."

As Farren left Doctor Gordon's house, he had never felt so scared and alone in his life. Looking back over the past eight months, was it an accident meeting Rebecca, and falling in love and her asking him to marry her all in one short week? She had not attended his school. Where was she from? What was she doing there, at the university when he received his law degree? Why had she thrown her arms around him and kissed him so deeply? Why had he let her talk him into this crooked mess? His family was very well off, he didn't need this stolen cattle money, or stupid cattle ranch, but he needed Rebecca. But wait, when was the last time she had been to bed with him, months? Everyone else had, everyone, but not him.

Throwing his money and clothes into a large traveling bag, he looked around his office. "Mildred, Mildred Gordon! Now she loves me! I'll take her with me! I'll not go to the ranch, but we'll go to Santa Fe. Yes, yes, the territories will hide us forever! I still have my law degree! I'll be the best lawyer in the west!"

Leaving his office with his first smile in months, he stopped in his footsteps as he saw Booger, Nate and two other fellows being pulled from their horses in front of the jail.

"My God! I've got to tell Rebecca! They'll be after her next! No, no, I'm finished. I don't care what happens to any of them! I'm getting Mildred and getting out of here while we can!"

"Oh darling, yes, yes I'll marry you! I'll tell my father, and we'll be married this afternoon. I have waited for this, so long."

Farren didn't hesitate for a moment. "No, dear. I want to leave for Santa Fe at once. We'll elope there, the moment we arrive. The stage leaves within the hour. Please throw some clothes together and I'll be back for you within thirty minutes."

"But, but, darling, my father must know. I don't want him to worry himself to death. Go, go my darling, I will be ready."

"Dear, we don't have time to tell your father. Some men were killed over at the jail, and he will be tied up for hours. Write him a note and tell him you are eloping. Don't tell him with whom, or where we are going. Later, after we are settled, we'll send for him. We all will get out of this lawless hell hole."

Mildred was on cloud nine. Humming to herself, she packed everything she had into two trunks, and one small handbag. After dressing, she looked at herself in the mirror.

She would make a beautiful bride. Oh, if only her father could be there. At last, total happiness. With the note written, she waited a minute or so, then decided being as Oliver wasn't back, she would run the note over to her father's house.

Doctor Gordon, had turned everything over to the undertaker, and went home to wash his hands, and eat breakfast. As he walked into his bedroom, Rebecca stood there, half naked, with a surprised look on her face. "Darling, take me to bed! Right now! I need you so bad it hurts!" Damn, he had walked in, catching her as she searched through his bedroom for his hidden money. She knew it was here somewhere.

Doctor Gordon had just gotten on top of Rebecca, as Mildred walked into the living room. Placing the note she had written, on her father's medical bag, she started for the door. Hearing groaning and moaning, she tiptoed to the bedroom door. Seeing her father hump Rebecca, red faced she back- tracked to the living room and sit down. Being as her father was here, she'd wait and tell him of her elopement plans. He must never know she caught them in the act. Oh how she hated Rebecca. She was a witch, and had taken her father from her.

She watched the big clock on the wall, wishing they would hurry and get it done and over with. She needed to get back to her room before her darling returned for her. She was so happy, but yet sad about having to leave her father.

Gator was still passed out from a night of drinking, and had just opened his eyes, looking around Farren's kitchen for a cup of strong coffee. Clothes were slung everywhere, furniture was upset and nothing was in order. Last night, the place had been spick and span. Something was sure in the hell wrong.

"Wonder where in the hell Booger and Nate went? Oh yeah, they was headed back to get Dean and that damn marshal. I'd better get some of the boys together and blow that damn jail to hell and back. I'd bet the fellers are about ready to get out of there. Yeah, that shouldn't take too long."

As Gator stepped to the street, he saw the undertaker's wagon leave the front of the jail. "Well hell, maybe some of my boys already drilled a couple dumb cowboys and busted Reyes, Jeb and Ned out of there."

Walking toward the café, Gator stopped the saloon slop boy as he walked down the walkway, and asked, "Wouldn't happen to know what's going on over to the jail, would you?"

"Yep, shor' do. Them fellers what was in there, done an' got their selves killed. Yep, all of 'em. I'm going to mop up the mess. The town pays me four bits for doing it."

Gator grabbed him by the nap of his neck. "Where in the hell is Farren? Did you see Booger and Nate before they rode out this morning?"

"No, shor' didn't see them 'fore they rode off this morning. But I did see them when they was brought back, all tied up and throwed in jail! Yep, they was four of'em. Bound and tied."

A small twitch of fear ran up Gator's spine. "Just who in the hell brought 'em in?"

"It was that Deputy U.S. Marshal, called Buffalo, and Dean Bessmer. Yep, it was."

"Dean! I should have killed that bastard while I had the chance! How would you like to make a quick twenty dollars?"

"Heck yeah! That's morn' I make in two months! Who do I got to kill? It can't be a friend of mine."

"Naw, you don't have to kill nobody. I want you to ride to Mullins old place and get about thirty of my men. Tell them to meet me west of town along the river. And tell 'em to bring ten sticks of dynamite. Oh just a minute."

Quickly writing something down on paper, he said, "Hand this to Jun Dung. This tells him to round up the other men and get the cattle headed for Hayes City. Be sure and tell him to push that herd hard and fast for at least three days. I figger there to be a posse coming after us, soon's we break Booger and Nate out of jail. We'll head south, then circle back around.

Might take us three or four days. Now you ride like hell, the cattle have to be on the move to-day. We'll bust the boys out tonight. And when you get back, keep your damn mouth shut!"

Rebecca left the bedroom first, and stopped dead still at the sight of Mildred. "And just what are you doing here, if I might ask?" These two women hated each other.

"If it's anything to you, I must see my fa-ther."

"Oh, he'll be out of the bedroom in a mo-ment. We were just humping for a bit. Do you ever hump? Oh, of course you don't. But it sure beats playing with ones self, doesn't it? But then again, you wouldn't know about that either, would you?"

Mildred was getting so mad, if not for her father, she'd scratch Rebecca's eyes out. She had to say something, even before her father came into the room. "Yes, Miss smarty pants! I know what you are talking about! I have had a lover for some time now, and we are going to elope!"

"Elope? You! Ha, who ever with, my dear?"

"Oliver and I..."

Rebecca almost screamed. "Oliver! Do you by any chance mean Oliver Farren?"

Doctor Gordon walked into the room. "Oliver Farren, what? What did he do?"

Rebecca was steaming mad, and found it hard to hold her composure. "Your daughter and Oliver are going to elope! Have you ever heard of anything so ridiculous?"

Doctor Gordon looked from Rebecca, to Mildred, before saying, "Yes, my dear. The most ridiculous thing was you and I being married. As much as I dislike Farren, he'll make Mildred a good living, and they might even be happy. Now Mildred, when will this be happening? We'll build you a home. We can..."

"No, Father, we are leaving within the hour. We are going to live in Santa Fe, New Mexico Territory. He can start a new practice there, and I will teach school."

Rebecca was already back in her bedroom, putting on her riding clothes. She was so damn mad she wanted to scream. "That ungrateful bastard! After all I've done for him! Why in the hell does he think I picked a lawyer to go through a fake business deal with? I thought my lover would make a great lawyer. I did that to keep us out of jail! Before I let him go, I'll kill him myself! I still need that law degree of his to get my ranch back!"

Buffalo felt good about catching Booger, and not killing him on the spot. Now, how was he going to pull Gator into a trap? He wanted Gator even more than Booger. It had been Gator who had shot his wife Kathline. "Shorty, we've got to guard this bastard with somebody more than a couple of cowboys. Nothing again cowboys, I just want somebody here that will shoot first and ask questions later. Oh, before I forget it, I clubbed Booger pretty good. His head is still swelling. Think we ought'a get Doc to take a look at him? I'd shor' hate for him to die this quick."

Shorty looked in on Booger. "Booger, you want the Doc to see you? Your head looks pretty messed up."

"No, just get the hell out, and get Farren over here!"

"Don't think he'll be able to help you much this time. Judge Walker will hold court come morning. Looks as if you'll finally get a bit of what's coming to you, you murdering bastard!"

A loud banging on the back door, brought guns from holsters. Judge Walker looked around and saw everyone was ready. "I'll open the door and step to the left side. Don't get me in the cross fire."

The door was flung open, and there stood Bufford. "Bufford, what in the hell are you doing knocking on the back door? Hell, we knew you were coming to mop up this mess."

"Yep, I knowed that. But Gator just give me twenty dollars to go out to Mullins old place and give this note to Jun Dung. And I was to bring thirty men back here with ten sticks of dynamite so they can blow up the jail. I figgered y'all would want to know it before I went and done it."

Shorty read the note. "Says here for Jun Dung to get the rest of Gator's men and head the cattle toward Hayes City, in a run. Well, Bufford, you don't have to go that far. Just you stay out of sight, and we'll handle things from here."

"No, Mister Shorty, I gotta take this here note out there. Gator done paid me the twenty dollars. I told him I would."

Shorty thought for a couple of minutes. "All right, you go ahead and take it. Just you forget to say anything about them bringing dynamite. Don't even tell them what Gator's got in mind. I believe we can set us up quite the trap. This might come off better and quicker than anyone thought."

Everyone started loading rifles and pistols. Dean asked where he and Buffalo should set up.

Jack Johnson asked if he could make a suggestion. "I figger this will make or break the backs of the ranchers in these parts. Between me and David, we got nigh on to eighty men. That ain't counting the towns men that will help us put up a fight. What I'd like to see is, for Dean to take about forty men and pull a running hit and miss on that cattle drive. If they can keep them old boys pretty busy, maybe they won't feel like driving them cattle very hard. And Shorty, we'll leave the trap setting here in town up to you. All we gotta do is be careful not to let Gator find out what we're doing. Everybody should be told to keep an eye out for him and if seen, bring him down with a bullet."

A whip cracked above the backs of the stage horses. Pulling hard, the stage left Tascosa in a cloud of dust. Hollering above sounds of pounding hooves, the driver tried to carry on a conversation with a new shotgun guard. "Willie, we ought'a be at old Fort Bascom right at sundown. It's nigh on to a sixty-mile trip, but we got good horses, and the road ain't half bad. Old Pablo Montoya's outfit has kept the stage office open since the army closed the fort. They shor' do feed us rather well."

The guard spit a half-cup of tobacco juice into the dust before saying, "I didn't know that any of Pablo's people was still alive. Don't John Watts have that land leased?"

"Yeah, but Pablo's kin still lives around there and helps run the ranch. Hell of a big spread."

By late morning, huge thunderclouds were building in the west and north. Heavy rains were more than a possibility. The stage driver had just let the horses get a good drink of water from a water hole that was fed by a small spring. "Willie, I shor' don't like the looks of them clouds. We could get our asses wet beforrr." A rider was on a horse, standing in the middle of the road with a rifle held across his lap.

Waving the stage on, the rider pulled to the side. As the stage passed, he fired three quick shots into the passenger compartment, before kicking his horse into a run, headed east.

Laying a rifle over the top of the stage, the guard fired one shot, and saw the rider slump slightly in the saddle. Stopping the stage, the driver got down to check on his passengers. "Anybody hurt back here?"

Farren spoke up first. "No sir, but I know that rider was trying to kill Mildred and myself. I must return to Tascosa and put a stop to their killing and the stealing of land and cattle. This has gone too far." Farren shuttered at the thought of how far they would go. "My family would think me a disgrace."

"Well feller, you can't go back unless you walk. I shor's hell ain't turning around. You might can buy a horse from Watts, or even one of them Montoya's, and go back tomorrow."

The stage started on to Fort Bascum. Mildred was very concerned. "If you return to Tascosa, my dear, I must return also. I could never go on without you. Perhaps we can buy or rent a buggy or carriage at Fort Bascum, from Mister Watts. We shall return together. Perhaps father will be able to help you with what ever you must do. I know he would understand better, about us going off to Santa Fe. Darling, I'm so touched that you will be helping the ranchers, instead of that Gator. I never liked him."

"Dear, I haven't liked myself for sometime now. That will now change, and I will live up to my family name."

CHAPTER TWELVE

"Hell, Doc, I don't know who shot her! I was coming from the N D Ranch for the dance tonight. She was just laying beside the road. Her horse was fifty feet or so over eating grass. I looked to the northwest and saw them rain clouds coming in pretty fast. I couldn't leave her there and come on into Tascosa for a buggy. Hell, she might have drowned!"

"Slim, I'm not faulting you for bringing her in, it's just why would anyone shoot Her? Rebecca has no enemies that I know of. It had to have been one of those men of Gators!"

Doc Gordon was very concerned about the bullet hole in Rebecca. When he removed the bullet, he saw her right shoulder was severely damaged. If she lives, she may never be able to raise her right arm again? "Lord why would someone do such a thing? Slim, I want you to tell no one about this. She is my wife, and I will take care of it. Will you keep this quiet for me?"

Doc had a pleading look on his face.

"Sure thing Doc. It was a bit too dark for anyone to see who she was. And Doc, I'm shor sorry 'bout this. Hope she makes it."

Slim closed the door and headed toward the saloon. Large raindrops had begun to fall. Damn, just made it before the rain. Bad as we need it, I shor do hate to get my ass wet on a hoss."

After breakfast, Gator had gone back to Farren's and waited for his men. Lucky for him, Farren still had plenty of food around. "Where in the hell did Farren get off to? When you need that bastard, he ain't no where to be found."

Gator kept pulling his watch from his pocket, checking the time. "That damn Buford! I bet he went and got his self lost! Why in the hell else wouldn't the fellers be here? Now this stinking rain! When we blow up the jail and leave here, they can foller our tracks plum' to hell and back!"

It was full dark when Gator made up his mind to go for a bottle. "Where in the hell could Farren got his self off to? Hell, I'll just walk to the end of the bar get my bottle and leave. I don't have to talk to nobody. The boys ought'a be here any minute now. A couple of bottles will help once we're in the saddle."

Paying the bartender, Gator looked all about, then asked, "Hadn't seen Farren around today, have you?"

"Not since mornin'. Him and the Gordon girl got on the Santa Fe stage together, just before it pulled out. Looks as if they pulled out, and ain't comin' back. Lotta bags. You need him?"

Gator looked the bartender in the eyes. "You shor he didn't leave with Rebecca?" Gator couldn't figure this whole thing out.

"Naw, naw, I'm shor wadn't tha Doc's wife. It was his daughter. Yep, I'm dead shor it was the Gordon girl all right. Nice shapely girl. Funny, I never noticed that before. Her shape, that is. Uh huh, that tight dress fit right well."

"I don't give a damn what you did or didn't notice! When my boys get here, you tell 'em that I said for them not to get dog assed drunk, and get over to Farren's house!"

"Hell Gator, I was just makin' conversation. Didn't know you was so pissed offfff... Ahhh shit!"

Gator had just seen the bartenders eyes go from a squint, to as large as a silver dollar. Then both heard the distinct sound of a hammer being cocked. The next feeling was the barrel of a rifle at the base of Gator's skull.

"If you so much as twitch, or a hair stand up on the back of your neck, I'll blow a hole in you so damned big I'll be able to stick that bottle through it! Barkeep, get your hands in plain sight, and keep 'em there! Now!"

Still moving his arms, the barkeep smiled, "Naw, naw, Marshal. You don't understand I was just going to blow...!" Buffalo shot him in the chest, as his hands came from under the counter with a sawed off shotgun.

Gator was quick to try his move, but a rifle butt to the back of the head knocked him as cold as a widow woman's heart. He lay on the floor in a crumpled heap.

Some of the men around the saloon had their hands on their guns, while others had hardly noticed and went on with their card games. Buffalo was wishing Dean would get here from the outhouse. He had been gone long enough to have fallen in.

"Any of you men here work for Snyder or Johnson?"

Buffalo knew he was going to need help at any moment.

Several men stepped forward. "Yeah, most of us in here do. What do you want us to do?"

"I want one of you to get me a rope, while the rest of y'all stand guard out front. I'd shor hate for any of his men to come riding into town about now. It'd be hard to see 'em coming in this rain. Most times this skunk don't travel alone. Probably wouldn't hurt if a couple of you boys went to the hotel saloon for Shorty, Dave and Jack. Think I'm gonna need 'em."

Buffalo still had his rifle cocked and pointed at Gator's back. "Ever which one of you boys are best at calf tying, get over here and use this rope. Make it good and tight. I don't want to have to shoot this bastard before he goes to trial."

Gator was tied, wrist behind his back and to his ankles. Buffalo reached for a luke warm pitcher of beer, and poured it right in his face. It still took Gator a couple of minutes before starting to move, and shake his head.

"Bob, go to the horse trough and bring a bucket of water. I'm bringing him to, I ain't gonna carry him to jail." Buffalo wanted so bad, to yank Gator by the hair, yelling about what he was going to do to him, but no, he'd wait.

Gunfire and the sound of running horses down a muddy street brought Shorty and the other men from the hotel bar. The jail was ablaze and the rain was little help in putting it out.

Jack headed for the jail, while Shorty went to see Buffalo in the Sandstone Saloon. "Buffalo, what in the hell happened?"

"Well, I went outside to see how bad it might rain, and saw Gator walk into this saloon. I got my rifle from my saddle and walked up behind him. The barkeep must have been one of his spies, 'cause he went for his shotgun and took a bullet for his trouble. Just now bringing Gator around. What in the hell was all that shoot'n out there a bit ago?"

"Damned if I know, but the jail is on fire. Jack, Dave and the town people are fighting it now. Come on, we'll put Gator somewhere with heavy guard while we see how bad the jail is burnt." Shorty looked around the bar.

"Hell, tie him to the porch rail and leave three men guarding him. We'll be back and get him later."

"Jack, what happened?" Shorty was looking at a dead man.

"It was Gator's bunch. They shot both my men and broke Booger, Nate and them other two out of here. They sneaked up on 'em. One of 'em said I sent him to relieve them for supper. When they opened the door, they got shot. Jasper is dead but Arron might make it. Has anybody gone for the Doc? And another thing, it's raining too hard to get on their trail tonight. And tracks will be washed out 'fore morning."

"Yeah but they ought'a be behind a large herd of cattle, headed for Hayes City." As much as the rain was needed, now was a bad time for it.

A knock on the door awoke Doc Gordon from a light dose. "Who is it?" He put his glasses on, before opening the door.

"Doc, it's me, Slim. They need you at the jail. There's been a killing and one man is wounded. When they said for somebody to come get you, I did, just in case you wanted me to stay with the lady while you was gone. I hadn't told nobody else."

"Thank you Slim. That's very thoughtful. I'll get my bag. She hasn't moved or regained consciousness yet, so I'm sure she'll be no problem. Water is on the stand, if she should need some. I'll return as soon I can. Again, thank you."

Arron was dead before Doc got to him. Both men needed a undertaker. Doc quickly excused himself and went back home.

Judge Walker and Shorty looked the jail over. One coal oil lamp had been thrown under the desk. Only the desk and a small portion of the floor had burned. The jail was still useable, and all the doors could still be locked.

"Boys, it don't look like this rain is going to let up tonight. It'd be best if we all got some sleep. We'll have a full day tomorrow. Mister Heard, think you can open your store early for us to get traveling supplies. We'll need a good bit."

"That'll be no problem ah'tall. Be glad to do it."

"Shit' I forgot about Gator! Get him Buffalo. Lock him up with four men sitting guard. Do you want to be one of them?"

"Yeah, I do. It's a damn shame about Booger getting away. Gator shor's hell won't. We'll sleep in shifts, two sleeping, and two guarding. Shor hope them bastard's come back for this two-legged sack of rotten dog shit. I'll get 'em all!"

Booger and the men that broke him from jail had no idea Gator was now in their place. Making a bad decision, Jun Dung had already headed the cattle north in this blinding rainstorm. Sixty men on horse back, started pushing over three thousand head of cattle toward Kansas. Sheets of rain made it hard to see more than a couple hundred feet. Everyone had a short, fast breakfast, before saddling horses, and pulling out rain gear. Outlaws don't like rain, much less driving cattle in it.

Everyone thought with morning light, the rain would slack up a bit. That was not the case. The clouds were as heavy as anyone could remember. Shorty and the other men sat in the café, even after breakfast was well over. Dean walked back from looking outside, saying, "Still rain'n like a cow pissing on a flat rock, and looks like its gonna keep it up awhile, maybe even all day. Think we ought'a wait to go looking for Booger and that bunch of cattle?"

David took another sip from his coffee cup before standing, and walking to the door. "Yeah, by now the river is too damn high for us to get safely across. If Booger and that damn china man are not plumb dumb assed stupid, they won't start a drive 'till the rain stops, or at least slows considerably. Hell, it's hard enough just to see across the street. Just think what it has to be like on the trail."

Everyone drank coffee and though of a time or two when he had been caught in blinding rain, or hailstorm just like this one.

CHAPTER THIRTEEN

"Doc, I'm sorry, but you'd better come alone with me and undertaker Underwood. We gotta go out to the San Jon Creek. Could be maybe a mile or two south 'fore it hits the river. Looks like a couple of people got caught in a flash flood while crossing San Jon Creek. Too dark for me to tell who they are. Time we get out there, maybe the rain will slack a bit. Better bring rain tarps."

Doc Gordon and undertaker, Jake Underwood, had taken Jake's wagon, instead of the buggy. Slim had insisted. Last night, the dance had been canceled, so Slim was headed back to the N D Ranch about four AM. He had come upon a buggy that had gotten caught in the raging water of the normally low running San Jon Creek. The buggy and two bodies were caught among the limbs of a huge cottonwood tree. The horses were not to be found.

Doc Gordon stood stone-faced, staring at the gruesome sight. "Yes, that's my Mildred and Oliver. What in the world were they doing in a buggy? They left Tascosa on the Santa Fe stage.

I can only think they might have been trying to return to Tascosa last night in the dark, and didn't see the flash flood roaring down the creek. Slim, if you'll hand them down, me and Jake will lay them in the wagon."

With a rope under their arms, Slim lowered Mildred first, them Farren. "Nothing personal Doc, but I ain't comin' back to Tascosa for a spell. Seems like I find bad trouble."

"No Slim, if not for you, we might have never known of any of this, Rebecca, or Mildred and Oliver. Buzzards would have removed any evidence within a few days. I am in your debt again. Thank you Slim. Me and Jake will get on back."

Slim kicked his horse into a long lope, and never looked back. He had seen more death this trip than ever before. "The damn west is becoming too crowded! Must be over two hundred people just in these parts ah' lone. I'd bet they is mor'n ten people or so for every hundred square miles. I'm staying on the ranch! Well, maybe I'll be back for the next dance."

Arriving back in Tascosa, Jake and Doc were soaked to the bone. The rain would slack up a bit, then return in torrents. They pulled the team under Jake's shed, and went about removing the bodies of Mildred and Oliver. Jake put his hand on Doc's shoulder. "Doc, I'll have 'em ready for burial anytime after the rain stops. And Doc, I'm shor' sorry about this."

"Thank you Jake. I'll be around later. I've got to get on home. My wife is very ill."

Booger hollered above the noise of rain and moving cattle. "Dung, we'd better call a halt, these cattle ain't gonna be drove much more! Hell, we ain't come mor'n two mile today. Maybe this rain will stop 'fore morning, and we can hit the trail early."

Jun Dung raised his eyes upward. "We must push on. Your law will be in close pursuit. Now that you have broken from their jail, they have what they have wanted for a long time, to be able to convict you of a crime. If you had waited, Gator would have gotten your release, legally, with the help of lawyer Farren. Now, where is Gator? He has not been seen since all of you were in Tascosa. And what if he has been caught by your law?"

"Hah! Gator caught! Not by them dumb nitwits! Gator's too damn smart for them. He'd never put his self where he'd get caught! Hell, he took us plumb to China, didn't he? They was just lucky when they got me and Nate."

"Is there a safe place to stop this big of a herd?" Jun Dung had never trailed with a herd before, and had no idea of the hazards of the west, or a lightening spooked herd.

Booger went about getting the men to circle the cattle into a manageable bunch. Other men set up camp, using several tents and large tarps. The cook wagon was in the center and had tarps extending from both sides and the rear. The smell of coffee had the outlaws standing around, waiting for it to brew. Several brought out bottles of whiskey, and passed them around.

Booger poured himself a cup of coffee, and looked at all the bottles being brought forth. "Fellers, I want y'all to go easy on the hooch 'til we get these cattle to Kansas. Getting' drunk out here could get you killed, and we could loose the whole herd."

Several men were moody, and wanted Booger to know it. "Look here, Booger, we didn't sign on to herd no cattle in a damn rainstorm! This wadn't in no deal we made. You know we been standing around for months gettin' nothin' but nickels and dimes. When you and Gator pay us what we got comin', you can tell us when to and when not to drink. 'Til then, go straight to hell!"

"Buster, just who in the hell do you think bought that booze you're drinking right now? I did by damned! Now you'll do as I say, or hit the damn trail!" Booger had to control the men.

"Just you tell who the damn idiot was that thought it wise to start this drive in a flood! Hell's fire, we could have waited at least 'til tomorrow morning! And, we'd sure as hell made better time!"

Booger had his hand on his gun butt.

"Damn it all to hell, Buster! There could be law comin' right now! Can't y'all get that through yer damned heads? Now shut the hell up, or get!"

"Now Booger, you know damned good'n well the law can't cross that river for another two days, maybe even three! This shit'n rains keeping up. These cattle will bed down right here and not move 'til this storm is over. I'm head'n back to the ranch and a dry bed for the night. Ever'body ought'a come along, we're no more'n two, maybe three miles from the ranch. These cattle know this country. They won't go off nowheres. We come back here in a couple of days they'll just be here eating grass. Hell, we may's well see if we can cross the river into Tascosa! A little punetang wouldn't hurt 'fore we hit the trail. Wait, wait just a damned minute! Dean's sister is still back there at Mullins place. I think I'll go on back there and drill her! Hells fire, Gator ain't around, and she shor' needs poke'n!"

"Buster, you know you can't cross that river, and yer damn shor' askin' for a bullet! Gator don't allow nobody foolin' around with his woman! You'd better find yerself a dry spot and finish that bottle here. Sleep it off, Buster. Best for everybody if you don't go off to see that woman."

"And you ain't my daddy, Booger! You can't tell me shit!"

Booger started to turn away, but spun back with his gun in his hand. "You ain't got a daddy, Buster!"

As the bullet slammed into Buster's belly, the sound of the shot started the cattle into a deafening, frenzied stampede. Riders at the north end had already turned the herd, pushing them into a tighter circle. The stampeding cattle came bellowing straight into camp. Men that were in tents knew nothing of the pressing herd. They had no chance to get to their horses. Twenty or thirty men that were standing under the tarps of the chuck wagon managed to grab their saddle horns and hang on for dear life. Some swung to their horse's backs, while others were pulled under slashing horns and hooves of the rushing cattle. As the chuck wagon turned onto its side, Jun Dung was frozen in screaming fear. The screaming stopped, as the life was crushed from his body.

Booger had been so damn mad at Buster, wanting to shut him up, he failed to think of the herd, or the men. Now he was being dragged with his right hand on his saddle horn, unable to get a foot into the stirrup, or pull himself into the saddle. Fear ripped through his mind as he wanted to stop the racing horse, but knowing if he did, the herd would trample them both. Pulling hard on the left rein, he managed to get the horse at an angle to carry them from the path of three thousand terrified cattle.

As they found an open path, and were in the clear, Booger knew he was now safe, but his horse stepped into a prairie-dog hole and stumbled head over heals.

Booger was flipped through the air as if he were a small child. As he landed, the horse was already down and thrashing about, trying to rise on a broken leg.

Booger had problems of his own. He screamed in pain at the sound of crushing bones in his right hip and leg. His thigh had snapped like a dry twig, as it pulled his hip socket completely apart. Flesh and skin lay open from the sharp, broken bones.

His screams went unheard by the fleeing men. In a matter of moments, the herd was gone, and all was quiet, except for the thunder, lightening and pounding rain. Booger reached for his pistol to fire a shot in the air. It was gone! His gun was gone, lost in all the panic! He must find his hat and cover his face. He was on his back, about to drown. Unable to move, or help himself, he was alone, three miles from Mullins old ranch, in a drowning rainstorm. How long would it take to drag himself three miles in all this mud? Surly the men would come back, looking for him.

"Bullshit, them bastards are miles from here by now! I know, Gator will be here by morning. Yeah, Gator will help me. We'll round up the herd and push on to Kansas. We'll be gone before...

what in the hell am I thinking? I gotta get to a Doctor! Hell's fire, I can't even sit a horse!"

Panic again clouded his mind. "Help! Help! Damn'it, why don't somebody come and help me?" Placing the crook of his elbow over his mouth and face, he kept his eyes closed. Maybe it would stop raining, and things would look better a little later this morning. "I'll just nap and rest up a bit. Gator ought'a be here! God, God, but this pain is killing me!"

Two hours passed before he tried to open his eyes. He was being turned on his left side, and he felt a hand go deep into his right pant pocket. "What, what in the hell are you doing? Can't you see I need help? Is Gator here? Who in the hell are you, anyway? Damnit, answer me! Oh shit, yer killing me! What in the hell do you want?"

A gun barrel smashed the side of his head, making his mind think he'd been shot. Darkness over took his brain. He was unconscious, lying face down in deep in mud.

"Damnit Delbert, he was suppose to have a gob of money on him! Look again! There, there! I told you so! Now lets get the hell out of here. Wait, wait, let's count it! Hand it to me! I want to know how much we got!"

"Jenkins, we'd better jest get! We'll head for Santa Fe, and count it somewhere along the trail. I don't want somebody ridin' up and see'n us. Gator would kill us both, and not bat an eye, if he thought we had his money. What if some of the other boys come back this way? Now's the time to high tail it out of this country, an' not ever look back. Sides that, I think you killed Booger. Looks dead to me, anyhow. He don't matter none though, but you might ought'a shoot that horse, its in pain."

CHAPTER FOURTEEN

The rain stopped late that afternoon. As the clouds parted, the sun seemed brighter than ever. Jack and David's men had sat around the saloon all day, drinking and playing cards. Shorty and Dean walked out to the river to see how high it was.

"You know, Shorty, we should have known by the sound that it was still too high. Maybe it'll be low enough in the morning for us to get after Booger and them cattle."

"Dean, we don't know that they've even started the drive yet. Hell, we might just have to ride to Mullins and get 'em there. We gotta take a bunch of gun hands with us. Them sixty or so fellers ain't gonna give up that herd very easy like."

"Shorty, I'm heading for Mullins place come mornin'. They still got my sister out there, and I'm gonna get her back. If they ain't started the drive yet, they'll be busy with me and y'all can maybe have a better chance of cutting 'em off."

Walking back in the saloon, Shorty heard Jack giving his men orders. "I want every man to hit the hay early tonight. We got one hell of a lot of ridin' to do tomorrow. If we get rid of all them rustlers, we'll take the cattle back to Mullins to separate by brands for the rightful owners to pick up. It's gonna be rough, so everybody get your guns cleaned and stash plenty of ammunition in yore saddlebags. Ain't no time to be runnin'short. And another thing, I don't want no man alone out there. Be in pairs."

"Damn, is that you Jun? Can't see too well right now. Seems I got mud in my eyes. Hell, I thought that stampede got you for shor'. Yer not just gonna stand there and watch me die, are you? After all I went an' done for you! Damnit say something! Give me some water so I can wash my eyes and face. My leg is broke, and I can't move too well, but you just give me a hand and I'll be good as new in a couple of weeks."

Booger was sitting in six inches mud and looked as if he'd been rolling around in it. "Ain't Jun, he's dead in that stampede. All yer men are dead or run plumb off, and the cattle are scattered from hell to breakfast. Told you assholes you ought'a waited 'til the storm was over! Now we gotta lot of gathering to do 'fore them ranchers come an' find their cattle scattered all over hell's half acre. How long you been laying out here, no way?"

Booger tried wiping mud from his eyes, but made it worse. "I don't know, since last night just about dark, I'd guess. That's when the stampede started. I damn near got clear, but that fool horse stepped in a prairie-dog hole. Shor' messed up my leg somewhat, but ole Doc Gordon can fix me right up. Now how about givin' me that water so I can wash this damn mud off my face? Then you can get me back to Mullins an' send after Doc."

"All right, I'll do that, but you won't be able to ride a hoss. Here, take a good drink an' wash yer face. I'll head back too the ranch and get a buckboard to haul you back. I'll also get the rest of the men to start gathering these cattle. You an' Jun Dung shor' messed up this cattle deal. "Ought'a let you lay here an' die. But I won't, yer still partners with Gator, an' I'd hate to get him on the sore side with me, I'd have to kill you both. Lay there, an' try not to move too much, I'll be back."

Booger drink long from the canteen then poured water into his hand, washing his face. As his eyes cleared he saw the man riding away on a big spotted horse. "Damn! Hells fire! That's Mullins! Son-of-a-bitch, he's who Gator said he'd made a deal with! That's who sent Gator that wire telling him… What the hell, I'm dead no matter how you look at it! Rotten, stinking dead! He just rode off without helping me, and won't be back, or even send anybody! That dirty rotten bastard!"

CHAPTER FIFTEEN

Sherilea Bessmer and Digger Jones lifted Booger slowly onto the back of the buckboard. "Digger, was it Mullins what sent you after me? I know it was him that give me that drink of water." "Yeah, it was him all right. First time anybody's seen him since we took over his place. Wunder wher him and his sons have been staying. Bet it was pretty close an' he knowed what was going on all along. Don't you think that, Booger?"

"Yes, yes! He had to have knowed, but damnit Digger, slow this damn buckboard up a bit. This damn shakin' is killin' me!"

Sherilea hadn't said a word, but when Digger turned to look at Booger, she grabbed his gun and shot him in the head. As Digger fell from the wagon to the ground, Sherilea had the reins in her hands, and Booger started screaming.

"Naw, naw, now Sherilea, you know I was always nice to you! What are you doing? God! Slow down, yer killing me! Oh God don't do this! You know I only raped you 'cause you wanted it! You know it's true, now slow down!"

Not saying a word, but clamping her teeth down tight, Sherilea slapped the horses on their rumps with the reins. "Yaw, yaw, get a move on, there! " Booger was bouncing all over the back of the buckboard, as She slapped the horses even harder. Sherilea knew, this time she had a chance to escape these rustling, raping, murdering skunks. The river was just ahead. They were in an all out run, headed for Tascosa. There was no one to stop her this time, no man, only the river!

Sherilea pulled back on the hand brake, and reins at the same time. The horses were on their rumps, sliding closer and closer to the raging floodwaters of the Canadian River. Only yards from the edge, the horses turned east, along the bank.

Finally stopping the horses, Sherilea sit with her eyes and mouth wide open. Booger grabbed her around the waist with one arm, trying to drag her into the bed of the buckboard. A gun barrel along the side of his head changed his mind. He was out cold again, sleeping like a baby.

Getting down, she walked the riverbank back and forth hoping someone from town would see her. Checking the gun for bullets, there were only five left. "If I fire three shots, someone might hear, but if they didn't, I'd only have two left to fight Booger's men with. I know, I'll get shells from Boogers gun belt, he won't miss em'. Damn, wrong calibur!"

Pulling off her shirt, she tied it to a long stick. She hoped no one could see far enough to see her breast. When someone walked outside a building for something, she'd wave her flag and holler at the top of the voice. After several tries, and it not working, she saw a fellow walk out the back of the saloon, heading for the outhouse. Aiming about two feet above the top of the outhouse, she fired a shot. Just as Shorty opened the door, the bullet hit a board with shattering noise.

Shorty was belly down, looking around the corner when the next shot dug up dirt ten feet away. Looking to the north he saw a person waving a flag on the other side of the river. Putting off taking a leak, he headed that way.

Getting to the south bank, Shorty shouted, "Yeah, what's your problem? You can't cross this water yet, it's too swift."

"Look, whoever you are, I know that! I ain't stupid! I need to talk with Dean Bessmer! I'm crossing this river in about fifteen minutes, safe or not, so you'd better get me some help. I've got Booger Boogs in the back of the wagon, and I'm gonna need help if some of his friends show up. Oh, so you'll know, he's all busted up and out cold right now, but hurry! Tell Dean I need him real bad."

"All right, you just hold on a minute or two. Oh, and put yer shirt on, I can see yer tits. I'll be back with Dean, or at least a lot of help." Shorty turned on his heels, headed for the saloon, but changed his mind and went into the outhouse to take that leak. Five minutes later fifty men lined the south bank of the river, shouting back and forth.

Sherilea looked down at her breast. "Hell, they don't look that bad! Maybe he was shy." She laughed out loud.

Dean hollered where Sherilea could understand him over the rushing water. "How did you get away? Where is Jun Dung? How did you get Booger?"

Sherilea was so frightened and angry, she didn't know how to shut Dean's mouth so they could help her across the river. "Shut up, Dean! Darn it all to heck! Those men will be after me as soon as they find out I didn't take Booger back to the ranch. Someone throw me a rope and I'll tie it to the horses and y'all can pull us across. Please hurry, oh please hurry!"

Dean turned to Shorty. "Shorty, what are we gonna do?

Nobody could throw a rope that far."

Shorty looked around. "I don't know what to do, but who has the strongest horse? I mean one that might could make it across."

David was as worried as every one else. "Damn Shorty, most every horse in Tascosa is a cow horse. Damn shame I don't have my pair of mules here, they could do it."

Judge Walker stood at rivers edge for several minutes then stated, "Wait right here! I'll be right back, I know what will work!"

He headed for mainstreet, and into the mercantile in a run. Grabbing a ball of twine, the owner started hollering. "Hey, hey there! Get the hell back here and pay for that!"

"No time, but I'll be back later!" Walker was back at the river's edge within a few minutes with the huge ball of twine.

Dean looked at the twine and ask, "Now just what in the hell are you gonna do with that? It sure as hell won't pull that buggy!"

"I'm going to tie a rock on it and throw this to your sister."

Dean shouted. "What the hell for? That won't pull that buckboard and horses across that water!"

Walker laughed out loud. "No it won't. But this twine is light enough to be thrown across. Once your sister has the twine, we will tie enough rope to this end, and she can pull it across. Then she can tie it to the buckboard and horses. All we need over here is several horses to take this end of the rope."

"Well I'll be a dumb assed frog! You sure as hell didn't learn that in no law school!"

"No Dean, that's what you call common sense."

Hollering back and forth, at last Sherilea had the ropes tied to the harness of each horse. Booger started groaning and trying to sit up. "You'd better sit yer ass down and hold on for dead life! If you get throwed from this buckboard, you'll sure as hell drown. Won't nobody risk even a dead horse to save yer sorry hide!"

Sherilea eased the horses into the water. They both reared and tried turning back. With a loud crack of the reins on their buts, they lunged forward. "Yaw, yaw, get up there! Pull you son of a mule, pull!" The buckboard was now in deep water and drifting down stream. Suddenly the ropes got tought, as the horses on the south bank started their pull. After a few frightful moments, the buckboard swung gently into the bank, with the horses digging in and pulling hard.

Dean vaulted into the wagon, throwing his arms around Sherilea. "Damn, but you are a sight for sore eyes! Honey, I tried mor'n once to get you out of there."

"I know Dean, I know." Sherilea was glad it was over. "Dean, will Doc Gordon be able to save Booger's life?"

"Well, yeah, he ought'a be able to, but why do you care if he dies or not? Looks like you'd want him dead."

"Oh, I do want him dead! I just want him to suffer a few years first. I would like to see them take him to the hanging tree, then back to his cell at least twice a day. Then every once in a while, just slip the rope around his neck, snug it down, then take it off."

"I don't know honey, there's one hell of a lot of people that just want him dead, no matter how." Dean helped her from the buckboard, as Shorty and David moved Booger where he could be lifted to the ground.

Buffalo came walking up, offering a hand. Grabbing Booger by his shirt front, Buffalo jerked him to the ground in a screaming, blubbering mess. "You ain't getting loose this time, ass hole!"

Two of Jack's men went to the mercantile and brought back a twelve-inch wide, two-inch thick board. Four men lifted Booger, while the board was slid underneath him. Taking turns carrying, the men soon had Booger in jail and lying on a cell bunk.

Doc Gordon was sent for, to look after Booger. Sam Kirkindall, knocked softly on the door. "Doc, oh Doc. They need you down at the jail. Sherilea brought Booger in, all bunged up. He looks pretty bad, and that U S Marshal said I'd best come and get you. Doc, Doc, I know yer home, an' we need help."

Doctor Gordon slowly opened the door, looking as if he hadn't slept in a week. "Sam, go back and tell them that I'll be down later. I'm tied up at the moment."

"But Doc, I…"

"Look, Sam, what difference does it make if I go now, or tomorrow. Booger will hang right along beside Gator in a few days. What could be the big hurry?"

"Doc, he's got a busted leg, with the bone sticking way out, and Sherilea split his head wide open in a couple of places. He's starting to stink pretty bad."

"All right Sam. Go by the saloon and take a couple bottles of whiskey over there. Give Booger one of them and tell him to drink it all. I'll be there in less than half an hour."

Doc went to the bedroom taking fresh water to Rebecca. "Dear, there has been an accident and a man has been hurt pretty bad. He has a broken leg and some head and facial abrasions. I might be a long while. I will send Mrs. Nelson to watch over you while I'm gone."

"No! I don't want any body coming in here! No one can see me looking this way! Don't ever let any one know what has happened. I just couldn't bare it! I'll… I'll, be all right. Just take your time and let on as if everything is all right. Please!"

"But dear, there are already questions as to why no one has seen you around lately. I have just told them that you are ill."

"Then keep telling them that. Nothing else."

"Yes, dear, I'll be back as soon as I can."

Doc turned to leave, but stopped with his hand on the doorknob.

Rebecca spoke in a low, almost inaudible tone. "Wilford, tell me the truth. Will I ever be able to use my shoulder and arm again? Will it shrink up and look all awful?"

Walking back, and sitting down on the edge of the bed, Doc Gordon reached for Rebecca's hand. "Dear, I just don't know. I am not that good of a surgeon. I can fix up knife wounds, remove bullets, set broken arms and legs, among various other things, but I can't go inside of your shoulder and do what needs to be done. There is muscle and tissue that needs to be reattached. That I just can't do. We'll talk when I get back."

With a sigh, he patted her hand. "I know a surgeon in Atlanta, Georgia that I'm sure can fix you right up. Think on it while I'm gone. As I said, we'll talk when I get back."

CHAPTER SIXTEEN

"I can not, and will not work on this man while he is lying on the floor! Bring one of the cell cots out here where I will have the most light, and plenty of room." Doc Gordon took a long swig from one of the whiskey bottles.

Jack watched the Doc, saying, "Never seen you do that before Doc, is everything all right?"

"Yes, yes, everything is just fine, except get twenty or thirty of these men out of here where I can work. Damn, you only have two prisoners, and one of them is dying."

Booger was drunk, but understood what Doc Gordon had said. "Now Doc, you fix up this leg and hip, and I'll be out of here in no time at all."

"Booger, you dumb shit! I'm fixing you up so you can walk up the steps to be hung! You are going to die one way or the other! You and Gator are a couple of murdering no good bastards! You are not getting out of this!" In his heart, Doc Gordon knew it was their bunch that had shot Rebecca. He had no idea it was the stage guard, when she tried killing Farren and Mildred.

"Damn, Doc, you sure are worked up today. Maybe you should have another snort from that bottle." Jack nor any one else had ever seen Doc Gordon act the way he was today.

"Jack, I have lost a daughter, and my wife is very ill. I should be with her instead of trying to mend a broken leg of a man that is going to hang. Three or four men can carry the bastard up the scaffold, tie a rope around his neck and throw him off!"

Buffalo was the only other man in the room that agreed with the Doc. "That's a damn good idea, Doc. We can have Judge Walker hold trial right now, convict the bastard and hang him all within ten minutes. Who's with me?"

"No one is with you, Buffalo. I know how much you and everyone else want to see these men hang, but that will have to wait. Being as Lawyer Farren got killed, there is no lawyer to defend these men. We will have to wait until Booger is able to travel, and send him and Gator to Austin for trial. There is no way they could receive a fair trial in Tascosa." Judge Walker was a judge of the people, for the people and would not stand for a lynching or mob to control his court.

"Now how in the hell do you expect them to be convicted in Austin, when nobody there knows what they've done? You and every other judge can just line up and kiss my ass! I'll kill both of these bastards before they can get to Austin!" Buffalo was like a raging buffalo. "These men killed Kathline, and will damn sure die for doing it. One way or the other, and no judge will ever be able to turn them loose. "You'd better hear me, no turning them loose!"

While Doc Gordon was working on Booger, Shorty caught Buffalo by the shirtsleeve to get his attention. "Buffalo, let's go over to the saloon, and have ourselves a drink. I need to have a talk with you about all this. You can't go around half cocked." Shorty knew Buffalo was about to explode.

Before walking out, he turned to Jack, "Jack, why don't you and David come along. I'm going to need y'all too."

The saloon was not all that busy, so they got their pick of tables. Everyone waited until after drinks were brought around to start talking. Jack was first. "What do you have on your mind, Shorty? Looks serious to me." Jack took a short drink.

"When do you think you'll be able to start after the cattle, where I can round up the rest of Gator's gang."

"Probably tomorrow, but it's still going to be rough. I'd say there is still another sixty or seventy men with Jung Dung. They ain't going to give up those cattle without a fight. But we can do it."

Dean had just walked in and heard what Jack had said. "May not be all that bad. Sherilea said Jung Dung was killed in the same stampede Booger got caught in. Most of the men that were on the drive didn't show back up at the ranch, so they must have scattered. There was a gob of 'em killed. The stampede happened at early night. Some of 'em were already in bedrolls."

Everyone took another drink or two while that soaked in. Dean continued, "Oh the other problem. She also said Mullins was alive and running the whole shebang. Nobody knows where he's been, he just showed up after the drive started."

"Damn! Is she sure about that?" Jack had known Mullins since he arrived in the Texas Panhandle, and just couldn't believe him going bad. Hell, his youngest son had been named Jack.

"Dean, where is Sherilea now? I'd like to talk with her about all of this." Jack thought for a moment. "Although, none of the Mullins' bodies was ever found, and nobody has seen them."

"Yeah, I took her over to the boarding house so she could get cleaned up and put on some new clothes. Them bastards kept her in rags so she wouldn't run off. Want me to go see if she's ready?"

"Naw, I'll go over there after me and Dave get the men ready to go after the cattle."

Buffalo was sitting there looking like a mad man. "Shorty, y'all go on about getting the cattle. I'm headed back to the jail and watch them two. I don't trust nobody, 'cept some of the men I know. There's one hell of a lot of people coming and going around there that I don't like."

Judge Walker walked in and pulled himself up a chair. "Buffalo, I heard what you said, and I agree with you. When Booger is well enough to travel, I want Jack and David to give me five men each, which I will deputize in the name of the U.S. Courts.

Then we, who is you and I, will see to the delivery, and safety of Booger and Gator to the courts in Austin. Then we..."

"As I said, no son-of-a-bitch in Austin has any idea what these bastards have done! Hell no! I'll gut shoot them right here and now! You'll not...! Now Buffalo was cut off.

"Buffalo! Damn but you are a hard headed... Look Buffalo, if you will let me finish what I was trying to say, maybe you'll understand better. Gator and Booger will not get off. Damn'it, they will not get off, they will hang, but by the law! Not your way!

I will be the prosecutor, you know, the Attorney for the court. I have the evidence, and the witnesses to send them to the gallows. You will be the number one prosecuting witness."

"What do you think, Shorty?" Buffalo was settling down.

"Buffalo, what he says is true. With him talking to the court in Austin, them two will be hung within two weeks from now."

"What about you, are you going along?"

"Hell yeah! I wouldn't miss it for the world."

Jack stood up. "All right, now that that is settled, I'm going to see Sherilea. Dean, come along. Oh, David why don't you get the men lined out? If you don't mind."

"Will your men take orders from me?"

"They sure as hell will, or they'll be looking for a job when I get back! Tell 'em I said so!"

Doc Gordon walked into the saloon and ordered himself a drink. With his elbows on the bar, he slowly sipped away. Most of the noise stopped, as man after man glanced at Doc, and then didn't take his eyes off him. Never had they seen Doc act this way.

Jack stopped before going out the door. Looking at Doc Gordon, he turned back to the bar. "Doc, something bothering you? You hadn't seemed yourself these past few days."

Doc set his glass down, and looked up at Jack. "Yes, Jack, as a friend, there is something wrong and I just can't figure it out. I've told no one about this, but Rebbeca has been shot."

"My God, Doc! When? How? Is she dead? Who did it?"

Jack was in shock. He couldn't understand why someone would shoot the doctor's wife.

"No, she's not dead. The night of the flood, one of the N D ranch hands found her lying beside the stage road between here and the New Mexico line. Why she was out that far is beyond me. Anyway, I assumed it was Gator, Booger, or one of their men that had shot her. I got Booger pretty drunk so I could set his leg, but he was adamant that they had nothing to do with it. Then who? Why would anyone shoot any woman, and especially Rebbeca? To my knowledge, she has never harmed anyone."

"Have you ask her? Do you think she would know?"

"No, I haven't, but now I must."

Jack walked out the door, as Doc finished his drink.

CHAPTER SEVENTEEN

Breakfast was over and the men were saddling their horses. Shorty talked with Jack and David. "Jack, what do you and David think about everyone of us taking the Mullins Ranch first thing. It might take a couple of week or more to round up all the cattle. I'd just like to get Mullins and see if he was behind all this."

Shorty wanted to get every outlaw in jail that was to be taken to Austin for trial.

"Yeah, that sounds good to me. Probably make it safer for everybody. At least we won't have to keep watching our backsides for more outlaws coming upon us from the rear."

"All right, everybody mount up. Dean I'd like you to ride up here with me and Jack. Now if everyone is ready… Hey, has anybody seem Buffalo?" Shorty didn't see his partner.

A cowboy from the bunch hollered. "Yeah, here he comes now. Looks as mad as hell to me."

"Shorty, I ain't going with y'all this morning. I'm staying here and watch Gator and Booger.

They'll not get away again."

"Damn, Buffalo, yer right. I plum' forgot about them two. Just don't get into no more screaming matches with Judge Walker. After all, he's on our side."

The river was at least two and a half feet deep, but not too swift for the horses to get good footing. Once the north bank was reached, they were kicked into a long gallop. Over seventy-five cowboys had their rifles and handguns ready. Today, would spell the end to a long spell of rustling and murder. With new law coming to the Texas Panhandle, the ranchers were bound and determined to keep this country safe for all families.

They topped a low ridge, before dropping down to Mullins Ranch. A few hundred head of cattle grazed off to the west. They must have been missed in the round up for the drive to Hayes City.

"Listen up everybody! We're going in shooting. Anyone that comes out with a gun in his hand, kill the son-of-a-bitch. If at all possible, I want Mullins alive. All right, let's hit 'em!"

Very few of the men that were on the drive came back to the ranch after the stampede. Most that had survived were scattered and leaving west Texas, or were gathering cattle. It didn't take but killing six or seven here at the ranch, before the others threw down their guns and raised their hands in the air.

"All right, where is Mullins?" Shorty had one of the wounded men leaning against the porch.

"Went after them cattle. Him and the rest of the boys are going to make a drive with what's left of the herd. At least what they can round up."

"When did they leave?" Jack was sitting on his horse, wanting to get on the trail.

"No mor'n two, maybe three hours ago. I was in that stampede, ain't gonna be no fun rounding them beefs up. They run plum' to hell and breakfast. Am I gonna live?"

"Yeah, at least long enough to hang. Jack, we're gonna need four or five fellers to tie these men up and take 'em to Tascosa. That wagon over there looks as if it can be used."

"Yeah, that'll be all right. I don't figger them fellers out there looking for cattle will be in any good-sized group. We ought'a come up on 'em two or three at a time. Being as we're not knowed by no outlaw, they'll just think we're some of them."

"Then let's ride. We ought'a have some of them before sundown. We'd better take food from here for dinner and probably supper." Shorty couldn't figure why a rancher with this much land and cattle would turn to rustling his neighbor's stock.

Every small valley or arroyo had hundreds of head of cattle grazing. They were rounded up and pushed toward Mullins Ranch. That's where the ranchers would sort them out by brands, and given to their rightful owners.

Noon came and passed without seeing a single rustler, but by now over a thousand head of cattle were on their way to Mullins. Jack rode up beside Shorty.

"What do you think, Shorty. Either no outlaws were left, or they took off with what was handy. Hell there might not be enough of 'em left to drive to big of a herd. Maybe they just took what they thought they could handle."

"Yeah, I'm looking at it that'a way. But wait look at this! A few hundred head appears to have been cut out and headed west. Now why in the hell would you suppose they'd do that? There ain't nothing west of here 'cept New Mexico Territory."

"Yeah, and they're headed straight for Dean Bessmer's Ranch! Well I'll be damned! Has anybody seen Dean in the passed couple of hours? Maybe he'll know what's going on."

Jack pulled his pistol, looking all around, as they were nowhere near any cattle he fired a shot in the air to get the attention of one of his men.

As the man heard the shot, he stopped his horse and looked Jack's way. Jack was standing in the stirrups, waving his hat. The rider headed for them in a run. "What's up, boss?"

"Red, have you seen Dean lately?

"Yeah, him and Buster circled back around to the east, and I saw 'em pushin' a good sized herd toward Mullins."

Jack looked over at Shorty, before turning back to Red. "Red, I need you to head Buster and Dean off, and tell 'em I need to see 'em, pronto like."

"Shor' thang, boss." Red spurred his horse into a run.

"Jack, you don't think this was any of Dean's doing? I mean heading these cattle toward his place." Shorty had a leg looped around the saddle horn.

"Naw I sure don't. But all these outlaws know that Dean is in with the ranchers, and not at home. Only his wife and kids are there, with a couple of hired hands. Maybe whoever is driving these cattle, might be thinking he can hole up there with several hundred head until we stop looking. Then they can drive them straight north into Kansas, before turning east to Hayes City. I don't know it's just a thought."

"Sounds like a damn good thought to me. Which way do we go? After the few hundred head, or north after the larger herd?"

"We'll wait 'til Dean gets here, but I'm thinking we'd better head for his place. No need in his wife having to put up with the likes of what's headed her way. If we ride like the devil is after us, we ought'a catch up with 'em driving the herd, way before they reach Dean's place. Least that's what I'm thinking."

Dean and Buster rode up, sliding their horses in the mud. "What's up Jack? Red said you was looking for us."

"Yeah, what do you make of this cattle trail headed for your place? Think they might be intending to lay up there for a while?"

"By damn they could be thinking just that. I can't tell for sure, but I'd say these tracks are about three hours old. Can't be mor'n fifteen or twenty men pushing this size herd. I'd guess we'd have a good chance of catching 'em 'fore they even get to my place. Are y'all ready to ride?" Dean was excited, and itchy to ride. He had already taken the tie down thong from his pistol, then putting it back and forth several times.

Jack was looking at the tracks, and thinking. "Buster, head back and pick up Red, and all the other men you can find. We may be headed for a showdown.

Shorty sure wished they had more men along. But then again, they might do well. After all the Mullins ranch had gone well. Not a one of David's or Jack's men had been injured.

With twenty-seven men, they took up the trail. Pushing pretty hard, five hours from now would tell the story. How many men, how many cattle? Can they catch up before reaching Dean's?

Doc Gordon changed Rebecca's bandage, and there was no infection. Things were looking much better. "Dear, I don't want you to worry, but you may as well know now. Mister Farren and Mildred were killed in a flash flood over at San Jon Creek. I have no idea when or why they got off the stage and were returning to Tascosa by buggy. It's beyond me how this could have happened.

"Do you remember being shot? And do you have any idea who would have done such a thing? Did you see who did it?"

"How could I have seen who did it, when I was shot in the back? I don't have eyes in the back of my head, you know!" Even though Rebecca was still very weak from her wound, her tone was as snotty as ever. "Why do you have to stare at me all of the time? I'm a cripple now and will always be a cripple, is that it? How can you doctor cowboys with broken legs, arms and backs? How can you treat gunshot wounds and make the men well, but you can't make me better? You want me a cripple so I will always depend on you! I know that's why you won't help me as much, isn't it!"

"Now dear, you know better than that. As I have said before, as soon as you are well enough to travel, I'll take you to Atlanta and have a surgeon friend of mine make you as good as new. He has the knowledge and instruments in their new hospital. Please dear, you must be patient."

"Get out! Just get out and leave me alone!"

Doc knew she didn't mean what she was saying. She was just scared and striking out at him because he was the closest. But, she has always seemed to be a bitter young woman. He picked up his bag and walked out the door. He had to check on Booger's broken hip and leg. Stopping by the saloon, he picked up two more bottles of whiskey. Disinfectant, that is what it was for. Inside and out, it cures a lot of ills.

As he got closer to the jail, he heard men hollering and hammers slamming into nails. Judge Walker was standing in the middle of the street, shouting to a carpenter to lean a roof beam a little more to the west.

Doc Gordon walked over beside the Judge and watched for a couple of minutes before asking, "What in the hell is all of the racket? I could hear you yelling for two blocks."

"We are adding on to the jail. Jack's men brought more outlaws in and from the way it looks, there will be plenty more in the next couple of days. What are you doing out?"

"I figured I'd better take another look at Booger. If I can't keep the infection down, he won't live to see a trial. And... everyone sure does want him to hang. I've never been in a town where so many people were out for revenge. But with good reason, yes, very good reason. Are you one of those, Judge?"

"Yes I am, Doc. That is the reason I cannot set on the bench and judge these men. I know I couldn't do it fairly. I am sure these are the men that are responsible for my uncle's death. Some of these men should hang, while others should get life in prison. Then again I'm sure there are some of them that should only spend a few years behind bars. If I were the judge, they'd all hang and that would not be justice."

Doctor Gordon looked at the judge. "Judge Walker, I believe you are a honorable man. It's a damn shame we don't have a lot more honorable men in west Texas."

"Oh but I think you do, Doc. Jack Johnson and most of his men. David Snyder, Dean Bessmer, the Bass family, the Shaffers, Stilwells, Preacher Ayers. My God, there are so many I can't name them all. Tascosa has just had more than it's share of rotten, unconformable men. There are those that will never be law abiding. Men of this caliber pray on the weak and uninformed. They do it by force, guns and large numbers. Money and greed is all that it is about. They want everything without working for it."

"Judge, do you know the man you are going to have to watch like a hawk? I mean the one out for the most revenge?"

"No, who would that be?"

"U S Deputy Marshal, Buffalo Blackburn. That man is full of hate and will not let these men go free, even if a judge sets them free. He will see that every one of them is dead. If justice is not swift, Buffalo will be. He will get his revenge. These men will die."

"I believe he will help take all these men to Austin, and be satisfied watching them hang. That is my belief."

"Hope you're right, Judge. I just hope you're right."

Two hours on the trail of the rustlers, and Red gave out with a yell, and waved his hat in the air. "Hey, will y'all look at this?"

"What do you think, Dean?" Everyone sit on their horses looking down at more cattle tracks.

"I'd say another eight or nine-hundred head tied in right here. And being as I'm guessing, I'd say another twenty-five men. Now I'm just guessing, but that's what it looks like to me."

Shorty was thinking fast, while looking at, and counting the number of men they had along. "Jack, David, maybe we ought'a hold off until we can send a rider for the rest of y'all's men. I'd hate to go busting in there and get most of us killed."

"Yeah, that might be a good idea." Jack was thinking of the safety of everyone there.

"Wait, wait a minute! I've got an idea."

Dean was going in whether anyone else went or not. "Let's send Red back to round up all the men he can find, and the rest of us can circle north, coming into my place where we can't be seen by nobody. We can still beat this herd to my place by several hours. With the ammunition we have along, and with what I've got at the ranch, I think we can not only hold 'em off, but I think we can beat 'em! We can set up barricades that they can't get through. Hell, I've even got a case of dynamite that we can set right where the riders will be coming through. They'll leave the cattle out by the pond, before riding on into the corrals and barns. They know I have two hired hands so they'll try to knock them off from the barns. We'll just be there first. Well, what do you think?"

Shorty looked at Jack and David. "You're right Dean. We can damn sure do it! How much ammunition do you have at the ranch? I mean, we are lable to need a bunch mor'n we got now."

"I've got enough to hold off a Indian attack for two weeks."

"Hell, then let's ride!" Turning north, the horses hit a run.

Red knew time was of the utmost importance. He must make it to Tascosa, and get back with all the men he could find. By the time he reached Main Street, his horse would be completely worn out. He'd have to borrow one for the return trip to Dean's ranch.

From a lathered, tired horse, Red jumped off in front of the saloon. Busting threw the bat-winged door, he hollered, "We're gonna trap the rest of them rustling bastards at Dean Bessmer's ranch! Shorty, Jack, David and ever other man we had on the range is headed that way now. They're gonna need all the help they can get. How many of y'all will ride with me?"

Forty something men stood as one, several taking their last swig of whiskey, or finishing their beer as they pushed back their chairs. Moss McCullan stepped forward. "Red, you get yerself a drink, while I saddle you another hoss. Tired as you are, that'n you rode in won't make it back."

"Thanks, Moss. I sure can shor' stand a stiff drink. I'll meet y'all at the water trough." The bartender already poured a drink, and handed it to Red. Men hollered, moving quickly, adding to the excitement in the air. They were getting the chance they had been waiting for. They would now have the upper hand.

Doc Gordon walked passed several cowboys as they watered their horses. "What's all the excitement about?"

"The rustlers are driving the stolen herd toward Dean Bessmer's ranch. Shorty and the ranchers are setting up a trap. They already cleaned out Mullin's place. Looks like old

Mullins is back and running the rustlers. That's hard to believe, ain't it Doc?"

"Yes, yes 'tis. Never thought Earl would turn again his own kind. Guess we'll never know how much harm greed can do. But you know, Dub, Earl never acted greedy. Shared, and helped everyone, and was always good to his men. It's a damn shame. He sure was building himself a damn good spread."

Judge Walker noticed and heard the commotion in front of the saloon. After hearing what was going on, he offered to stop construction on the jail so those men could ride with the rest.

"Judge, I think it'd be best if you kept several of them right here working. If we get 'em all alive, you ain't gonna have the room to put 'em." Red threw another drink down, waiting for Judge Walker to make up his mind, as what to do.

"You're right, Red. I think I'd better send a fast rider to Fort Union over in the New Mexico Territory for the Cavalry. Maybe they can help us transport the whole bunch to Austin. Mean time, we can hold them in the livery, with ten or twenty armed guards."

Coming in from the northwest, Dean had led the ranchers to his place, undetected by the outlaws. The trap was now being set.

While the men were taking care of that, Dean got his wife and kids into the storm cellar where they would be safe from all gunfire.

Several buckets, half full of nails were set upon two rocks, right in the path the outlaws had to take getting to the house. A half stick of dynamite was put under each bucket, between the rocks. A rifleman for each bucket was out of sight with, a bead on the dynamite. All hell was going to break loose.

"I can hear cattle bawling. They ought'a be here in a bit! Everybody get set and let Dean fire the first shot. We want 'em well in between the dynamite before we start our push." Shorty edged out of sight into his spot in the loft of the barn. He, David and Jack had the best locations and would be able to see everything that happened. They were to fire on any rider that wasn't caught with flying nails. No outlaw was to get away.

The next hour was like a week for the waiting ranchers. The cattle were being pushed into corrals, which were located several hundred yards to the southwest of the barns and house.

Mullins and two of his men rode around to the east, then turned north, straight for the front porch of the house. "Don't see them hired hands of Dean's. Don't suppose they're not here, do you?" Mullins and the men were looking back and forth between the barns, riding in easy like.

Dean saw the outlaws had split up and

knew Mullins was headed for the house. While their heads were turned toward the barn, Dean made it in the back door of the house.

Stopping at the hitch rail, Mullins looked over his shoulder at his two men. "Y'all sit tight and keep a eye open. I figgered we'd already had to kill a couple cowboys 'fore now. It's ah' cinch they ain't off lookin' after cattle! Hell, we done went an' stole 'em all! Haw, haw, haw!" Dismounting, Mullins felt the butt of his .44, but didn't draw it from the holster. After all, Dean's wife wouldn't remember who he was.

Dean, glimpsing from a window, knew the setup. Standing behind the door as it opened, he cocked a double barrel shotgun. Mullins stopped dead still as heard the hammers click. Not turning to see who had a gun on him, he chuckled.

"Now, now little lady, we mean you no harm. We was just looking for Dean, and didn't see nobody around, so I come on in."

"Well I ain't no little lady, and I sure as hell mean to do you a bunch of harm! Turn around, slow like and shuck that iron at the same time. I'd hate to have to cut you in half right here, and have you bleed all over my floor."

"Dean, Dean boy! What's your problem? This ain't very neighborly of you now. I know I been gone awhile, but you do recognize me, don't you?"

"Yeah, I recognize your sorry hide...!"

Several dynamite blasts went off at almost the same time. Dean, not thinking, bolted for the door to see how good of a job was done on the outlaws. Mullins hit him behind the head, driving him through the open door and onto the porch.

Men were screaming, as horses bucked and tried to run from the barrage of nails that that cut them to pieces. One horse at the hitch-rail was down, slowly kicking it's last death throws. Mullins grabbed the other one by the reins. The outlaw in the saddle, with his mouth and eyes wide, as if trying to scream, slowly let go of the saddle-horn and slipped to the ground. Several nails were buried head deep in his back. Some had gone in straight, while others had gone in sideways.

Mullins, with his left boot in the stirrup, the horse spinning, and his left hand on the saddle horn, swung into the saddle. Jerking the reins to turn the horse, he didn't see Dean swing a board at the side of his head. Nor did he feel anything, as he was knocked to the ground, face down. Dean stopped the horse from rearing, and spinning and settled him down. Taking the rope from the saddle, he sat in the middle of Mullins' back as he tied him tight. "Get out of this you dirty rustling, murdering bastard!"

The remaining gunfire sounded far off, but Dean could see smoke come from gun barrels that were less than a hundred feet away. He shook his head to clear the dynamite blast that still rang loudly in his ears.

Shorty, along with Jack, Dave and their men, were walking among the dead and dying horses. When a shot was heard, everyone knew it was another horse being destroyed. Of the twenty-seven remaining outlaws, only eleven of them were unwounded. Only a few of the wounded would live through the day. Gunshots and nails had done a good job. Two of Jack's men and three of David's, had minor wounds. All would survive and be able to work again.

"Dean, looks as if your idea worked. We lost no men, and got everyone of these stinking bastards. And, most of all your family is safe. You're a hell of a lot smarter than you look." There was a moment of silence, as that soaked in. Jack was grinning.

"What tha hell do you mean, smarter than I look?"

"Kiddin' Dean, just kiddin." Everyone got a good laugh at the look on Dean's face.

"All right now Dean, think we can use a couple of your wagons to haul the wounded to Tascosa?"

"Yeah, but if you think it better, I have enough rope. We could just make their feller partners drag 'em along behind."

Shorty spoke up for the first time. "That

don't sound like a bad idea, but we're going to have to wait. You have to wait and get your revenge in Tascosa, along with everybody else. They'll all go in front of Judge Walker. I just hope the hell he don't send 'em all to Austin."

An hour later and they were ready to ride. "Dean, I know you're ready to go along, but I think you'd better keep five or six men here and y'all get this mess cleaned up. 'Fore you got back, you'd sure have a yard full of stink. Yer wife probably wouldn't like it no mor'n mine would."

Dean looked around at the more than a dozen horses that would have to be hauled off. "Yeah, suppose yer right. We can hitch up a couple of teams and drag 'em over north to that dry arroyo and dump 'em in there. The coyotes and wolfs will have enough to eat and maybe they'll leave my calves alone. But by damned I'll see y'all tomorrow in Tascosa."

The river had subsided even more and they had no trouble taking the wagons of wounded outlaws across. Shorty, looking straight ahead, and not speaking to any one in particular, said, "Damn, but I feel sorry for Doc Gordon. With this bunch here, he won't get a wink of sleep tonight. Hell, it's plum' dark thirty, now."

Red rode up as Shorty was saying what he had. "Don't think he'll loose that much sleep.

PAUL L. THOMPSON

All of 'em are dead, 'cept two. And Dean must have done a good job on Mullins. He's just now coming to. Bet he thinks a horse kicked him in the side of the head."

Jack eased back to talk with Mullins. "Earl, what in the hell was you think'n when you started all this?"

After waiting a few minutes with no answer, Jack rode back to the front. "I tried talking to him, but he ain't talking back."

CHAPTER EIGHTEEN

It was after midnight when Doc Gordon walked into his bedroom. Rebecca was reading, and looked up with a smile. "My, my, but aren't you the late one. Have you been out drinking or patching up some drunk? You're going to ruin your health if you keep this up. None of those men are worth your health."

Doc set his bag down, and poured water from a large white pitcher, into a matching washbowl. After washing his face and hands, while drying off, he walked to the bed. "Why the concern dear? Having a change of heart? Did you need a drink of water while I was gone? Or... did you just now figure out that if I die, you don't have a chinamans chance at a Baptist reunion?"

"Wilford!!" Tears seeped from the corner of her eyes. "I am so sorry for all that I've put you through. You have been everything a woman would want, and I have been nothing but an unthankful, spoilt child. Can you ever forgive me? I would love to try and make you a wife. Even if my shoulder does, or does not get better, even if the surgeon can't help me. I still will try very hard."

"We'll talk more on it in the morning. I am just too bone tired to think straight right now. Do you need anything before I turn in?"

"No thank you. Just you rest well. And we will talk later."

The smell of bacon and frying eggs brought Doctor Gordon slowly awake. At first he couldn't think where he might be, but when his eyes were fully open, he sat up with a start. "My God, who's fixing breakfast?"

Dressing in a hurry, he rushed into the kitchen to find Rebecca at the stove, and the table was already set for breakfast.

Seeing him with his mouth open, Rebecca smiled and poured him a cup of coffee.

"You awoke just in time. Your breakfast is ready."

Setting the food on the table, she poured herself a cup of coffee and sit down across from Wilford. "I told you I would try, and from now on, life around here will be better."

"Yes. Yes I know what you said, but I didn't think it would be this quick. I hate to say this, but I'm almost in shock."

"Yes Dear, and I can understand why. But don't worry, from now on everything will be all right."

"That sounds wonderful to me. Now, the

reason I was so late last night, is because the rest of the Gator and Booger gang was brought in. Several of them were wounded. What beats all to me is, it looks like Earl was behind this all along."

Rebecca sat forward in her chair. "By Earl, you surely don't mean Earl Mullins, by chance, do you"?

"Yes, that's exactly who I mean, and..." A firm knock at the front door interrupted Wilford in his speech. Excuse me Dear, I'll get that. It could be important."

Sherilea Bessmer was standing on the porch, looking to be in pain. "Come in, come in Sherilea. What seems to be the problem? You look a bit pale."

"Doc, I'm sorry to come this early, but I could hardly sleep last night. I've got these bruises that are driving me crazy. They hurt so bad, I'm afraid something might be broke."

"It will be a few minutes. My exam room is in a mess. Why don't you go into the kitchen and have a cup of coffee with my wife while I clean it up?"

"Gee, Doc, I thought your wife was dead."

"Oh, well yes, but I am married again. Just you go on in there and introduce yourself. Have a cup of coffee and I'll be ready for you in a little while."

Sherilea stepped through the kitchen door, and stopped dead still. "As I live and breathe,

Mary Ann Mullins! My God girl, where have you been for so long?"

Rebecca was in total shock at seeing Sherilea. "Sherilea, I am no longer Mary Ann Mullins! I am Rebecca Gordon. Please. Oh please keep my secret! No one must know for a good while. In front of Wilford, please act if we just met. I'll tell you all about it later, I promise. Please do this for me, please?"

Sherilea still had her mough open. "Sure thing Mrs. Gordon. I'll get my own coffee. Would you care for another cup?"

"Yes, thank you Miss. Bessmer."

Sherilea sat, not knowing what to say. "I see you have a bandaged shoulder. Was it from an accident?"

"Yes, I was shot."

"Shot! Damn, but I bet that hurt! I've never been shot before, but that damn Gator and his bunch has kept me locked up out at the Mullins Ranch. They beat the shit out of me a lot. Boy howdy they used me more than I thought a women could ever be used."

Puzzled, Rebecca half smiled. "Used, what do you mean?"

"I mean used like a two bit whore, that's what I mean. Gator was supposed to keep me for himself, but when he was gone, any of them big bastards would come in and rape me. Sometimes more than three or four a night."

"My goodness that had to be plumb awful.

I mean completely horrible. I don't know how you could have stood it."

"It was ruff'ern hell, but the thought of revenge made me even stronger. One hell of a lot of them ole boys are already dead, and a bunch more of them will lose their balls before they hang."

"Oh my God! You'd do that!"

"In a heart beat and a half. All I need is the opportunity. And I'll get it, someway, somehow. They'll pay for raping me, if it's the last thing I do!"

Rebecca looked toward Wilford's exam room, but he wasn't finished cleaning. "Was one of the men that raped you, Earl?"

"No, I never saw him until a couple of days ago. And Mary, shit, Rebecca, you ought'a know this, that really don't look like your dad. I know, I know, everyone, including him calls him Earl. But dad-gum-it, I knew your dad and that ain't him!"

"I know he isn't, that's... Wait, here comes Wilford. Come back and see me when he goes to the jail to take care of those men. Will you be sure and do that for me?"

"Sure, I'll be back. We've got some taking to do."

"Well Sherilea, nothing is broken, but you need to come back before you leave town and I'll change these wrapping for you. Now your breast, as well as your ribs are very brused and will be sore for sometime to come. Just be careful and try not to get hit in that area. Another large jolt could crack a rib or two."

"Thanks Doc. I'll be around town for several days yet. At least until the hangings, them I've got to see."

"Oh, then you didn't hear. Judge Walker has sent for the calvary so all these men can be transported to Austin for trial. It seems as though these are the men that killed his uncle, which was a Texas Ranger. It would be unethical for him to sit in judgment of the men that killed his kin."

"Unethical my ass! They don't even need a judge to say they're guilty! I say hang the rats right now, without a trial!"

"Now Sherilea, I know just how you feel, but we are trying to bring law and order to the panhandle and I think Judge Walker will do it. That little U S Marshal, Shorty Thompson will help."

"Doc, you have no idea how I feel! I'm going to get my revenge right here in Tascosa!" She walked out the door in a huff. "Austin! No damn way!"

Sherilea headed for the boarding house. Being so mad she could hardly see straight, she bumped into Dean as she started in the door. "Sherilea, where have you been? Damn, you had me worried sick."

"I've been over to see Doc Gordon. My

ribs and tits are so damn sore I thought something might be broke. Dean, you've got to help me."

"Anything, honey, you know that."

"Okay, you're going to help me castrate Booger, Gator, Elliott, and..."

"Naw, naw, now hold on Sherilea! I'll do no such thing, and nether will you! Are you crazy?"

"You damn right I'm crazy! Everytime one of those bastards climbed on top of me, the thought of cutting his nuts out was the only thing that kept me from killing myself. Dean, I'm going to do it! If you're not going to help, just stay the hell out of my way!" Sherilea stormed off, leaving Dean standing there with his mouth open. He had seen her mad before, but never like this.

Shorty and Judge Walker stepped into the new cell area of the jail. "Glen, we need to be alone with these prisoners for a bit. Will you see that we are not disturbed?" Judge Walker had a serious look on his face.

"Shor' thang, Judge. Just you holler when you want to come out. I'll be right outside this door."

The hallway between the new cells was about six feet wide, too wide for a prisoner to grab hold of anyone outside their cells.

Earl Mullins stood at the bars with a mad, twisted face. "What in the hell do you want in here? Where in the hell is Farren? I know we can see our lawyer. It's the law!"

Neither Judge Walker nor Shorty had batted an eye. "Well Mr. Mullins, I am very glad that you know the law. "First of all, Lawyer Farren was killed in that flash flood we had. Being as there is no other consul for you and your men, here in Tascosa, I have sent to New Mexico for the calvary to help escort all of you to Austin for trial. What I can figure out is, why, as a pretty wealthy rancher, would you turn to crime against your own neighbors?"

"And I answer to you, it's none of your damn business! Calvary, or no calvary, I ain't hung yet! Don't you bet any money that I will be! Now get, and leave me alone. I've got some thinking to do." Mullins turned his back and sit down on a cell bunk.

Shorty walked out behind the judge. Kind'a cock sure of his self, ain't he. Wonder what he's got up his sleeve."

"I surely don't know, but that is a very dangerous man. He is worse that a caged animal. I believe he would harm or even kill his fellow cell mates if it would give him a chance to break out."

"Yeah, I kind'a figgered that too. These men that feed, and take them to the outhouse, had damn sure better be careful. These next few days, until the calvary gets here, is going to be rough."

As they walked from the cell area, Doc Gordon stepped in. "Judge, Shorty, how does everything look?"

"Mighty fine Doc, but you be damn careful and have a armed guard with you everytime you go back there."

"Yes, I know. The guard lets me into the cell, then he closes the door and steps back to the office area."

"That's good Doc. These bastards are desperate!"

Sherilea stopped by the clothesline and got a wooden clothespin. Knocking on Doc Gordon's back door, she waited for Rebecca to answer. "Damn, I thought you might be back in bed."

Rebecca smiled. "No, I've been in bed too darn long as it is. Sherilea, I am so ashamed, I don't know if I'll ever be able to hold my head up in public again."

"What do you mean? What in the hell have you done?"

"This is a long story, but I'll make it as short as I can. I know you remember when my mom died, and dad sent me back east to live with my aunt and uncle. That's the last time I saw you. How old were we? Maybe twelve?"

"Yeah, I'd just turned twelve and you was gonna be in two months. But go ahead with what you were saying."

"Well my Aunt Martha and Uncle Merle

were not glad to have me stay with them. Uncle Merle was a vicious, vicious man. He beat me every chance he had, and my aunt would not lift a finger to stop him. On my twenty-first birthday, I got a letter from my dad for me to come home. I didn't find the letter until almost five months ago. Wait, I'm getting ahead of myself. Six months ago, Uncle Merle said he was going out west to see if he could find a ranch to buy. I wanted to come along, but he wouldn't let me, but said he'd send for Aunt Martha and me as soon as possible.

"About a month later, Aunt Martha stepped into the street and got ran over by a team of horses, and was killed. As I was going through her things, I found this letter from my dad. He couldn't understand why I wouldn't come home. This was the fifth letter he had written. Sherilea, I never got a one of them.

"Uncle Merle and Aunt Martha had told me that my father and brothers had been killed in a range war. Anyway I found another letter and it was from Uncle Merle. He had written to let Aunt Martha know that he had killed my brothers and my dad. He was now in control of dad's ranch, and was gathering more cattle to take to market. When that was done, he would come back and get her and they would go to California. He never said one word about me. I was so frightened and mad; I didn't know what to do. I had just read in the paper where they were having a graduation for lawyers at this college, and I knew I would need a lawyer. I found this big nice looking fellow and starting flirting. Two days later we headed for Tascosa."

"You mean the lawyer that drown in the flood was your lawyer? You were married!" Sherilea could hardly believe it.

"Yes, he is the man I came west with, and no I hadn't married him. When we found out some of the things that was going on here, he got tied up as the outlaws lawyer. I married Wilford, because he was on the town council and I could get information. I've treated Wilford so bad when I think of it; it most breaks my heart. He has been nothing but the most sweet, caring man I've ever known. I hope it's not too late to make it up to him."

"Damn, Mary, er, Rebecca, what are you going to do about Merle killing your pa? I know he's in jail with the rest of the gang."

"I know it, dang it, I know it, but what can I do? He is in jail and I'm sure I couldn't get to him. I do so want him to see me and let him know he isn't getting away with it."

Sherilea smiled. "Honey, you just stick with me. I'll show you how I'm going to get everyone of those bastards that raped me. Oh yes I am, and will they be surprised! Then we'll work on Merle, if he isn't a blithering idiot by then."

"Oh my God, you are serious, I can tell it in your eyes! Why are you playing with that clothedpin?"

"Oh, that ole thing? I just found it on your clothesline. It is my life saving weapon. I'll use this to kill several of those skunks. By the way, do you have a very sharp butcher knife that I can use? It really must be very, very sharp."

"I don't know, we should. Look in that top drawer. What are you going to use the clothespin for? How is it going to save your life? Sherilea, I don't understand one thing you are saying."

Sherilea laughed. You will, honey. Believe me, you will."

For the next three days, Sherilea watched as every man was taken from the jail to the outhouse. Early on the morning of the forth day, Gator was the first to sit down to take a dump. The guards were standing with their shotguns cocked and ready.

The blood-curdling scream that came from inside the outhouse scared the living daylights out of both guards. With his pants still down, Gator broke the door down as he lunged forward. Tripping on his britches, he lay in the dirt, bleeding, kicking and screaming his head off.

The guards stood there with their mouths open for several minutes, just watching him squirm. "Damn, Milton, his damn balls are gone! Help me get him back to his cell and we can get the Doc. God, look at this sucker bleed."

Milton came out of shock and grabbed Gator under one arm. "Damn, boy howdy, that's gotta hurt something fierce, huh?"

Shorty, Judge Walker and Dean Bessmer was in the cell area when Doc Gordon rushed in. "Now what in the world is going on here? With these men here, I'll never get a minutes peace."

"Doc, his nuts are gone!" Shorty was looking at Gator through the bars.

"Nuts gone! How in the world did that happen"

"We don't know. Thought maybe you could tell us."

"Get me some hot water and a few more towels. This is one hell of a mess. Shorty, send someone after some whiskey, he's gonna need some."

Buffalo was leaving the livery, and watched as Sherilea climbed out of the river, dripping wet, and removed her clothes before jumping back in.

Buffalo ran for the riverbank as fast as his legs would carry him. Diving in, he grabbed Sherilea around the waist and started to swim to shore.

"Let me go, you big dumb ox! Damn it, let

me go!"

"Ma'am, no need drowning yourself. Nothing can be that bad. Everything will work its self out."

"Bullshit! I ain't drowning myself you idiot! I was just going for a morning swim!" They were now standing in hip deep water. Buffalo had on his clothes, but Sherilea was naked.

Sherilea did have nice looking breast, and that's where Buffalo had put his sights. "Lordy, Lordy. Ma'am! I'm so sorry! I just thought... well I saw you take off your clothes and jump in the water, and just thought... Oh hell, lady, I'm sorry. And you don't have any clothes on and I'm looking right at your breast."

Sherilea smiled. "Yes, I noticed that you were. Shocked?"

"Well, I guess I am. Hell, I thought I was saving your life."

"You may have Mister. You just might have."

"What are you talking about? You already said you wadn't drowning. How in the hell did I save your life?"

"Well you jumped in the river to save a person you knew nothing about. Then when you saw me naked, you didn't just grab a hand full and have your way."

"No Ma'am, I could never do that. To beat that, you're a pretty lady. Wait a minute! You're Dean Bessmer's sister!"

"Yeah, does that make a difference? Now

that you know those bastards have used me, you'd have let me drown! I just wouldn't have been worth it if you'd known ahead of time, is that it? Well, is that what you're saying?"

Sherilea had her hands on her hips, and was spitting mad, as Buffalo slowly pulled her to him and kissed her softly on the lips.

Sherilea had her eyes closed as Buffalo released his embrace. She opened her eyes and said, "Damn, did you know we're out here in the middle of this damn river kissing, and I'm naked as a Jay Bird? Would you get me my clothes before someone sees us and makes a big thing out of it?"

"Oh, yes Ma'am." Buffalo retrieved her clothes and standing in the river, she started to dress. When the clothespin dropped from her shirt pocket and started floating away, Buffalo grabbed it.

"What in the world is this?"

"Oh, that? It's a clothespin."

"I know it's a clothespin, what's it doing in your shirt pocket?"

"It's for my nose."

"Sherilea, what in the hell are you talking about? You've got a pretty nose. What do you need that clothespin for?"

"Did you hear a blood-curdling scream a little bit ago?"

"No, I was over at the stable, taking care of my horse."

"Oh God, you've got to hear this from me! When the guards took Gator to the outhouse awhile ago, I had this clothespin on my nose and was down in the bottom of the outhouse, and..."

"In the bottom of the outhouse! What the hell for?"

"If you'll shut up long enough, I'll tell you! Anyway, when he sit down to take a crap, I cut off his balls!"

"You what?"

"Yeah, I cut off his balls and tried to get his tally-whacker, but he had it in one of his hands. That bastard will never rape another woman. I saw to that, and that is only the start of my revenge in Tascosa. Just you wait and see."

"Damn, Sherilea, I think that is just great, but how in the heck did you come up with that idea for revenge?" Buffalo was dumbfounded, but very proud of her.

"Well, with all of them in jail, I knew there was no way I could get to them in there, so I watched the outhouse to see when the guards took them to do their thing. I'm just so happy it was Gator, first. I only have three more of those skunks to go."

"You mean only four of them raped you?"

"Heck no! There was up to a dozen, but the others are dead. Oh, being as we kind'a know each other, you'll keep this quiet until I get the others, won't you?"

"Heck yes! I just wish I was small enough to fit down that hole myself, and give you a hand."

They both started laughing, as Buffalo walked her toward the boardinghouse. "Sherilea, I'm glad we got to talk, even if I didn't save your life." They laughed again.

"Well Buffalo, if you promise to kiss me every time you try to rescue me, I'll go swimming naked more often."

"You wouldn't!"

"Just you keep one eye on that river."

They both laughed again, and Sherilea pulled his head down and kissed him on the cheek. By, Buffalo, and thanks."

"Anytime, pretty lady, anytime."

This was the best Buffalo had felt in over two years. He hurried over to the jail to get the latest on Gator.

Doc Gordon was just leaving the cell area, as Buffalo walked in full of questions. "What happened, Doc?"

"Looks like when Gator went to take a crap, some animal tore off his balls. It was probably a wharf rat, for as much damage as was done. Wharf rats have got very sharp teeth. Damn shame it didn't pull him all the way down in that hole and eat him alive."

"Yeah it is. But he will live to be hung, won't he?"

"Yes, I don't see why not. Infection could

stop a hanging."

"You mean if it killed him first, that would stop the hanging!"

"That's right, Bufallo, that's right. If you need me, I'm home."

As Doc Gordon walked into his frontroom, he heard Rebecca all the way from the kitchen, screaming in laughter. Never had he heard her laugh so hard. "Well Sherilea, I am very glad you came back to visit with Rebecca. Never have I heard her so happy."

"Oh Wilford, I am happy. Thank you for sending Sherilea back here to the kitchen for coffee. If not, we would never met."

Sherilea was sitting there with an ear-to-ear grin.

"Well, you ladies go right ahead and visit. I have work to do in my office. Just asking Dear, will you be fixing dinner, or will I?"

"I will Hon, and Sherilea will stay and help me."

As Doctor Gordon went on about his business, Rebecca reached over and patted Sherilea on her hand. "Sherilea, I am so happy. Thank you for being here. I feel as though I can live again. And you want to know another thing? Since I have been back, you are the only woman I have spoken more than ten words to. And to beat that, we want the same thing, revenge, and we'll get it. Thanks mostly to you. You are so brave."

Sherilea smiled. "Brave I don't know about. Pissed off I do."

"I don't mind, but when did you start cussing so much?"

"I guess when those men had me, and I thought there was nothing I could do for myself. Maybe it gave me the strength to not kill myself and start thinking of revenge. That's what I'll attribute it to anyway." They both laughed, them smiled at each other.

"What do you say we fix Wilford the best meal he's had since his first wife died?" Rebecca reached for an apron.

"That sounds good to me. I haven't been eating to well lately myself. Gator and them wouldn't let me cook, afraid of poison."

They started laughing and chatting, while working away.

David and Jack, plus three other ranchers, had most of their men out rounding up cattle. It was decided the land and homes that were taken back from the outlaws, and now vacant, could be used by anyone that wanted, until a relative showed up. Then everything would revert back to that family. Including any improvements. That way the land would not set idle and weeds take over. It would also keep anyone from coming in to squat.

Over the next few days, while waiting for the cavalry, Tascosa settled down to a busy little country town. The only excitement was a different prisoner every morning, loosing his balls to rats.

After the next prisoners refused to use that outhouse, the town council had another hole dug and used two horses to pull the outhouse over the hole. Sherilea didn't care she already had all the balls she wanted anyhow.

The cavalry arrived about three in the afternoon. They brought along several wagons with bars on the windows and door. Two of them had to be reworked for the prisoners without balls, as they were not able to sit in a sitting position for very long. The cavalry doctor took a very long at the rat bites, before taking Doctor Gordon aside for a long talk.

"Huh, uh. And you told everyone that rats were biting off their nuts. Do you really think that possible?"

"No, but are you going to tell them it was a sharp knife from down in the bottom of the outhouse?"

"Hum, I see what you are saying. No, no, we'll leave things as they are. But, any ideas to who ever did it?"

Doctor Gordon smiled. "Yes, I sure do have my own ideas."

"One thing about it, for the next two weeks, those men will be in about as much pain as when it happened." You know, we'll be pulling out in the morning, with all of the prisoners?"

"Yes, and I thank God its over. They've run rough-shawed over this country for about a half a year. And we... here's the stage, we might as well walk over for any news."

The driver threw down the mail pouch, before he and the guard started handing down luggage. Three men and one lady stepped down and glanced around the quiet little town of Tascosa.

The driver saw Shorty walking up with Judge Walker and hollered. "Hey Marshal, I've got you another dispatch from the President. Say's here to hand deliver right to you."

"Yeah, its probably eating my rear-end out for not sending him a report about whats going on out here." Shorty took the dispatch and leaned against the hitch rail to read it.

"Damn, has anybody seen Buffalo?"

Melvin Martin stepped over to Shorty and softly spoke. "Yeah, him and Sherilea are down by the river."

"Well Melvin, would you mind going out there and tell him that I need to have a talk with him?"

"No Sir, Marshal. I'd be glad to."

Ten minutes later, Buffalo and Sherilea walked around front of the jail and caught Shorty's eye. "You needed to talk?"

"Yeah, I just got this dispatch from President Hayes telling me to head for Fort Union, over where this cavalry bunch is from.

It says I've got to go to Loma Parda. I'll talk with the Captain of these fellers and see if he can tell me anything. Anyhow, I ain't going with y'all to Austin. I already told Judge Walker."

Buffalo would normally have had a running fit, but instead said, "that's all right Shorty. I'd like to have gone with you, but I'm going to see both Gator and Booger hang. And by the way, Sherilea is going along. She's going to testify against all of them outlaws. After talking with Rebecca, and we all talk with Doctor Gordon, I imagine the Doc and Rebecca will go along."

"Why in the world would they make a trip like that?"

"Oh, you don't know, nor does the Doc yet, but Rebecca is really Mary Ann Mullins. Earl, who really isn't Earl, but who is Merle, is her uncle. Did you get that?"

"No, but don't tell me again, my head is messed up as it is."

"Okay I won't, but Merle Mullins is from back east, and came out here and killed his twin brother Earl and took over his ranch."

"The hell you say! Damn, brother killing brother, and I thought we had problems. Well everyone I know came here for revenge in Tascosa, but it looks like it all will take place in Austin."

Sherilea glanced right quick at Buffalo, as she was saying, "well, some revenge was got right here in Tascosa."

"Hum, you don't say? Could that have been cynide, of maybe even rats in the outhouse?" Shorty had a smile on his face.

"We'll never know, will we Marshal Shorty?"

"Not by me we won't. Come morning I'll be riding for Fort Union and Loma Parda, New Mexico Territory. Got me a whole new case to start on."